Austin Dobson

Vignettes in rhyme and vers de société

Now first collected

Austin Dobson

Vignettes in rhyme and vers de société
Now first collected

ISBN/EAN: 9783337259853

Printed in Europe, USA, Canada, Australia, Japan

Cover: Foto ©Andreas Hilbeck / pixelio.de

More available books at **www.hansebooks.com**

VIGNETTES IN RHYME

AND VERS DE SOCIÉTÉ

(NOW FIRST COLLECTED)

BY

AUSTIN DOBSON

HENRY S. KING & CO.,

65 CORNHILL AND 12 PATERNOSTER ROW, LONDON.

1873.

TO

ANTHONY TROLLOPE,

THESE VERSES

ARE GRATEFULLY INSCRIBED.

(Go, little Book, on this thy first emprize :

If that thou 'scape the critic Ogre-land,

And come to where young Beauty, with bright eyes,

Listless at noon, shall take thee in her hand,

Tell her that nought in thy poor Master stirs

Of art, or grace, or song,—that is not Hers.)

CONTENTS.

	PAGE
A Dead Letter,	1
A Gentleman of the Old School,	10
A Gentlewoman of the Old School,	18
Une Marquise,	26
The Story of Rosina,	34
A Revolutionary Relic,	47
Before Sedan,	55
Avice,	58
A Dialogue from Plato,	63
An Autumn Idyll,	67
A Garden Idyll,	76
Tu Quoque,	83
' Le Roman de la Rose,'	87
Ad Rosam,	90
The Love-Letter,	97
A Virtuoso,	102
Laissez faire,	107
A Legacy,	110
To Q. H. F.,	112

	PAGE
A Gage d'Amour,	116
Outward Bound,	121
To ' Lydia Languish,'	125
Growing Gray,	130
Love in Winter,	133
Pot-Pourri,	135
Dorothy,	138
A City Flower,	142
Incognita,	146
My Landlady,	152
The Drama of the Doctor's Window,	156
An Unfinished Song,	169
The Sundial,	173
The Sick Man and the Birds,	178
The Death of Procris,	182
Palomydes,	185
A Song of Angiola on Earth,	187
A Flower-Song of Angiola,	191
A Song of Angiola Dead,	195
A Song of Angiola in Heaven,	199
The Dying of Tanneguy du Bois,	204
The Bookworm,	208
The Peacock on the Wall,	211
NOTES,	217

A DEAD LETTER.

' *A cœur blessé—l'ombre et le silence.*'—H. DE BALZAC.

I.

I DREW it from its china tomb ;—
    It came out stained and dusky,
Still haunted by some thin perfume
    That, years ago, was musky.

An old, old letter,—folded still!
    To read with due composure
I sought the sun-lit window-sill
    Above the gray enclosure,

A

That, glimmering in the sultry haze,
  Faint-flowered, dimly shaded,
Slumbered, like Goldsmith's Madam Blaize,
  Bedizened and brocaded.

A queer old place! You'd surely say
  Some tea-board garden-maker
Had planned it in Dutch William's day
  To please some florist Quaker,

So trim it was. The yew-trees still,
  With pious care perverted,
Grew in the same grim shapes; and still
  The lipless dolphin spurted;

Still in his wonted state abode
  The broken-nosed Apollo;
And still the cypress-arbour showed
  The same umbrageous hollow.

Only,—as fresh young Beauty gleams

    From coffee-coloured laces,—

So peeped from its old-fashioned dreams

    The fresher modern traces ;

For idle mallet, hoop, and ball

    Upon the lawn were lying ;

A magazine, a tumbled shawl,

    Round which the swifts were flying ;

And, tossed beside the Guelder rose,

    A heap of rainbow knitting,

Where, blinking in her pleased repose,

    A Persian cat was sitting.

' A place to love in,—live,—for aye,

    If we too, like Tithonus,

Could find some God to stretch the gray,

    Scant life the Fates have thrown us ;

' But now by steam we run our race

 With buttoned heart and pocket ;

Our Love's a gilded, surplus grace,—

 Just like an empty locket.

' " The time is out of joint." Who will,

 May strive to make it better;

For me, this warm old window-sill,

 And this old dusty letter.'

        ’

II.

' Dear *John* (the letter ran), it can't, can't be,

 For Father's gone to *Chorley Fair* with *Sam*,

And Mother's storing Apples,—*Prue* and Me

 Up to our Elbows making Damson Jam :

But we shall meet before a Week is gone,—

 " 'Tis a long Lane that has no Turning," *John !*

' Only till Sunday next, and then you 'll wait

　　Behind the White-Thorn, by the broken Stile—

We can go round and catch them at the Gate,

　　All to ourselves, for nearly one long Mile ;

Dear *Prue* won't look, and Father he 'll go on,

And *Sam's* two Eyes are all for *Cissy, John!*

' *John*, she 's so smart,—with every Ribbon new,

　　Flame-coloured Sack, and Crimson Padesoy ;

As proud as proud ; and has the Vapours too,

　　Just like My Lady ;—calls poor *Sam* a boy,

And vows no Sweet-Heart 's worth the Thinking-on

Till he 's past Thirty,—I know better, *John !*

' My dear, I don't think that I thought of much

　　Before we knew each other, I and you ;

And now, why, *John*, your least, least Finger-touch,

　　Gives me enough to think a Summer through.

See, for I send you Something !   There, 'tis gone !

Look in this corner,—mind you find it, *John !* '

III.

This was the matter of the note,—-

   A long-forgot deposit,

Dropped in an Indian dragon's throat,

   Deep in a fragrant closet,

Piled with a dapper Dresden world,—

   Beaux, beauties, prayers, and poses,—

Bonzes with squat legs undercurled,

   And great jars filled with roses.

Ah, heart that wrote !   Ah, lips that kissed !

   You had no thought or presage

Into what keeping you dismissed

   Your simple old-world message

A reverent one.   Though we to-day
  Distrust beliefs and powers,
The artless, ageless things you say
  Are fresh as May's own flowers,

Starring some pure primeval spring,
  Ere Gold had grown despotic,—
Ere Life was yet a selfish thing,
  Or Love a mere exotic.

I need not search too much to find
  Whose lot it was to send it,
That feel upon me yet the kind,
  Soft hand of her who penned it;

And see, through two-score years of smoke,
  In bygone, quaint apparel,
Shine from yon time-black Norway oak
  The face of Patience Caryl,—

A Dead Letter.

The pale, smooth forehead, silver-tressed ;
　　The gray gown, primly flowered ;
The spotless, stately coif whose crest
　　Like Hector's horse-plume towered ;

And still the sweet half-solemn look
　　Where some past thought was clinging,
As when one shuts a serious book
　　To hear the thrushes singing.

I kneel to you ! Of those you were,
　　Whose kind old hearts grow mellow,—
Whose fair old faces grow more fair
　　As Point and Flanders yellow ;

Whom some old store of garnered grief,
　　Their placid temples shading,
Crowns like a wreath of autumn leaf
　　With tender tints of fading.

Peace to your soul ! You died unwed—

Despite this loving letter.

And what of John ? The less that's said

Of John, I think, the better.

I.

He lived in that past Georgian day,

When men were less inclined to say

That ' Time is Gold,' and overlay

    With toil their pleasure ;

He held some land, and dwelt thereon,—

Where, I forget,—the house is gone ;

His Christian name, I think, was John,—

    His surname, Leisure.

II.

Reynolds has painted him,—a face

Filled with a fine, old-fashioned grace,

Fresh-coloured, frank, with ne'er a trace

Of trouble shaded ;

The eyes are blue, the hair is drest

In plainest way,—one hand is prest

Deep in a flapped canary vest,

With buds brocaded.

III.

He wears à brown old Brunswick coat,

With silver buttons,—round his throat,

A soft cravat ;—in all you note

An elder fashion,—

A strangeness, which, to us who shine

In shapely hats,—whose coats combine

All harmonies of hue and line,

Inspire compassion.

IV.

He lived so long ago, you see ;

Men were untravelled then, but we,

Like Ariel, post o'er land and sea

  With careless parting ;

He found it quite enough for him

To smoke his pipe in 'garden trim,'

And watch, about the fish tank's brim,

  The swallows darting.

V.

He liked the well-wheel's creaking tongue,—

He liked the thrush that stopped and sung,—

He liked the drone of flies among

  His netted peaches ;

He liked to watch the sunlight fall

Athwart his ivied orchard wall ;

Or pause to catch the cuckoo's call

  Beyond the beeches.

VI.

His were the times of Paint and Patch,

And yet no Ranelagh could match

The sober doves that round his thatch

    Spread tails and sidled ;

He liked their ruffling, puffed content,—

For him their drowsy wheelings meant

More than a Mall of Beaux that bent,

    Or Belles that bridled.

VII.

Not that, in truth, when life began

He shunned the flutter of the fan ;

He too had maybe ' pinked his man '

    In Beauty's quarrel ;

But now his ' fervent youth ' had flown

Where lost things go ; and he was grown

As staid and slow-paced as his own

    Old hunter, Sorrel.

VIII.

Yet still he loved the chase, and held

That no composer's score excelled

The merry horn, when Sweetlip swelled

Its jovial riot ;

But most his measured words of praise

Caressed the angler's easy ways,—

His idly meditative days,—

His rustic diet.

IX.

Not that his 'meditating' rose

Beyond a sunny summer doze ;

He never troubled his repose

With fruitless prying ;

But held, as law for high and low,

What God conceals no man can know,

And smiled away inquiry so,

Without replying.

X.

We read—alas, how much we read!—

The jumbled strifes of creed and creed,

With endless controversies feed

      Our groaning tables;

His books—and they sufficed him—were

Cotton's ' Montaigne,' ' The Grave ' of Blair,

A 'Walton '—much the worse for wear,

      And ' Æsop's Fables.'

XI.

One more,—' The Bible.'   Not that he

Had searched its page as deep as we;

No sophistries could make him see

      Its slender credit;

It may be that he could not count

The sires and sons to Jesse's fount,—

He liked the ' Sermon on the Mount,'—

      And more, he read it.

XII.

Once he had loved, but failed to wed,

A red-cheeked lass who long was dead ;

His ways were far too slow, he said,

   To quite forget her ;

And still when time had turned him gray,

The earliest hawthorn buds in May

Would find his lingering feet astray,

   Where first he met her.

XIII.

' *In Cœlo Quies* ' heads the stone

On Leisure's grave,—now little known,

A tangle of wild-rose has grown

   So thick across it ;

The ' Benefactions ' still declare

He left the clerk an elbow-chair,

And ' 12 Pence Yearly to Prepare

   A Christmas Posset.'

A Gentleman of the Old School.

XIV.

Lie softly, Leisure ! Doubtless you,

With too serene a conscience drew

Your easy breath, and slumbered through

The gravest issue ;

But we, to whom our age allows

Scarce space to wipe our weary brows,

Look down upon your narrow house,

Old friend, and miss you !

I.

SHE lived in Georgian era too.

Most women then, if bards be true,

Succumbed to Routs and Cards, or grew

Devout and acid.

But hers was neither fate. She came

Of good west-country folk, whose fame

Has faded now. For us her name

Is 'Madam Placid.'

II.

Patience or Prudence,—what you will,

Some prefix faintly fragrant still

As those old musky scents that fill

      Our grandams' pillows ;

And for her youthful portrait take

Some long-waist child of Hudson's make,

Stiffly at ease beside a lake

      With swans and willows.

III.

I keep her later semblance placed

Beside my desk,—'tis lawned and laced,

In shadowy sanguine stipple traced

      By Bartolozzi ;

A placid face, in which surprise

Is seldom seen, but yet there lies

Some vestige of the laughing eyes

      Of arch Piozzi.

IV.

For her e'en Time grew debonair.

He, finding cheeks unclaimed of care,

With late-delayed faint roses there,

      And lingering dimples,

Had spared to touch the fair old face,

And only kissed with Vauxhall grace

The soft white hand that stroked her lace,

      Or smoothed her wimples.

V.

So left her beautiful. Her age

Was comely as her youth was sage,

And yet she once had been the rage;—

      It hath been hinted,

Indeed, affirmed by one or two,

Some spark at Bath (as sparks will do)

Inscribed a song to 'Lovely Prue,'

      Which Urban printed.

VI.

I know she thought ; I know she felt ;

Perchance could sum, I doubt she spelt,

She knew as little of the Celt

    As of the Saxon ;

I know she played and sang, for yet

We keep the tumble-down spinet

To which she quavered ballads set

    By Arne or Jackson.

VII.

Her tastes were not refined as ours,

She liked plain food and homely flowers,

Refused to paint, kept early hours,

    Went clad demurely ;

Her art was sampler-work design,

Fireworks for her were ' vastly fine,'

Her luxury was elder-wine,—

    She loved that ' purely.'

VIII.

She was renowned, traditions say,

For June conserves, for curds and whey,

For finest tea (she called it 'tay'),

And ratafia;

She knew, for sprains, what bands to choose,

Could tell the sovereign wash to use

For freckles, and was learned in brews

As erst Medea.

IX.

Yet studied little.   She would read,

On Sundays, ' Pearson on the Creed,'

Though, as I think, she could not heed

His text profoundly;

Seeing she chose for her retreat

The warm west-looking window-seat,

Where, if you chanced to raise your feet,

You slumbered soundly.

X.

This, 'twixt ourselves.   The dear old dame,

In truth, was not so much to blame ;

The excellent divine I name

   Is scarcely stirring ;

Her plain-song piety preferred

Pure life to precept.   If she erred,

She knew her faults.   Her softest word

   Was for the erring.

XI.

If she had loved, or if she kept

Some ancient memory green, or wept

Over the shoulder-knot that slept

   Within her cuff-box,

I know not.   Only this I know,

At sixty-five she 'd still her beau,

A lean French exile, lame and slow,

   With monstrous snuff-box.

XII.

Younger than she, well-born and bred.

She 'd found him in St. Giles', half-dead

Of teaching French for nightly bed

And daily dinners ;

Starving, in fact, 'twixt want and pride ;

And so, henceforth, you always spied

His rusty 'pigeon-wings' beside

Her Mechlin pinners.

XIII.

He worshipped her, you may suppose.

She gained him pupils, gave him clothes,

Delighted in his dry bon-mots

And cackling laughter ;

And when, at last, the long duet

Of conversation and picquet

Ceased with her death, of sheer regret

He died soon after.

XIV.

Dear Madam Placid ! Others knew

Your worth as well as he, and threw

Their flowers upon your coffin too,

I take for granted.

Their loves are lost ; but still we see

Your kind and gracious memory

Bloom yearly with the almond tree

The Frenchman planted.

UNE MARQUISE.

A RHYMED MONOLOGUE IN THE LOUVRE.

' Belle Marquise, vos beaux yeux me font mourir d'amour.'
MOLIÈRE.

I.

As you sit there at your ease,

O Marquise!

And the men flock round your knees

Thick as bees,

Mute at every word you utter,

Servants to your least frill flutter,

' Belle Marquise!'—

As you sit there growing prouder,

   And your ringed hands glance and go,

And your fan's *frou-frou* sounds louder,

   And your ' *beaux yeux* ' flash and glow ;—

Ah, you used them on the Painter,

            As you know,

For the Sieur Larose spoke fainter,

            Bowing low,

Thanked Madame and Heaven for mercy

That each sitter was not Circe,

   Or at least he told you so ;—

Growing proud, I say, and prouder

   To the crowd that come and go,

Dainty Deity of Powder,

   Fickle Queen of Fop and Beau,

As you sit where lustres strike you,

            Sure to please,

Do we love you most or like you,

        ' *Belle Marquise !* '

II.

You are fair ; O yes, we know it

       Well, Marquise ;

For he swore it, your last poet,

       On his knees ;

And he called all heaven to witness

Of his ballad and its fitness,

       ' *Belle Marquise !* '—

You were everything in *ère*

(With exception of *sévère*),—

You were *cruelle* and *rebelle*,

With the rest of rhymes as well ;

You were ' *Reine*,' and ' *Mère d'Amour ;* '

  You were ' *Vénus à Cythère ;* '

' *Sappho mise en Pompadour*,'

  And ' *Minerve en Parabère ;* '

You had every grace of heaven

  In your most angelic face,

With the nameless finer leaven

   Lent of blood and courtly race ;

And he added, too, in duty,

Ninon's wit and Boufflers' beauty ;

And La Vallière's *yeux veloutés*

       Followed these ;

And you liked it, when he said it

       (On his knees),

And you kept it, and you read it,

       ' *Belle Marquise !* '

III.

Yet with us your toilet graces

       Fail to please,

And the last of your last faces,

       And your *mise ;*

For we hold you just as real,

       ' *Belle Marquise !* '

As your *Bergers* and *Bergères*,

Iles d'Amour, and *Batelières ;*

As your *parcs*, and your Versailles,

Gardens, grottoes, and *rocailles ;*

As your Naiads and your trees ;—

    Just as near the old ideal

            Calm and ease,

As the Venus there, by Coustou,

   That a fan would make quite flighty,

Is to her the gods were used to,—

   Is to grand Greek Aphroditè,

         Sprung from seas.

You are just a porcelain trifle,

     ' *Belle Marquise !*'

Just a thing of puffs and patches,

Made for madrigals and catches,

Not for heart-wounds, but for scratches,

     O Marquise !

Just a pinky porcelain trifle

　　　　' Belle Marquise ! '

Wrought in rarest *rose-Dubarry*,

Quick at verbal point and parry,

Clever, doubtless ;—but to marry,

　　　　No, Marquise !

IV.

For your Cupid, you have clipped him,

Rouged and patched him, nipped and snipped him,

And with *chapeau-bras* equipped him,

　　　　' Belle Marquise ! '

Just to arm you through your wife-time,

And the languors of your life-time,

　　　　' Belle Marquise ! '

Say, to trim your toilet tapers,

Or,—to twist your hair in papers,

Or,—to wean you from the vapours ;—

　　　　As for these,

You are worth the love they give you,

Till a fairer face outlive you,

   Or a younger grace shall please ;

Till the coming of the crows' feet,

And the backward turn of beaux' feet,

         ' Belle Marquise !'—

Till your frothed-out life's commotion

Settles down to Ennui's ocean,

Or a dainty sham devotion,

         ' Belle Marquise !'

v.

No : we neither like nor love you,

         ' Belle Marquise !'

Lesser lights we place above you,—

   Milder merits better please.

We have passed from *Philosophe*-dom

   Into plainer modern days,—

Grown contented in our oafdom,

   Giving grace not all the praise ;

And, *en partant, Arsinoé,*—-

   Without malice whatsoever,—

We shall counsel to our Chloë

   To be rather good than clever ;

For we find it hard to smother

   Just one little thought, Marquise !

Wittier perhaps than any other,—

You were neither Wife nor Mother,

              ' *Belle Marquise !* '

THE STORY OF ROSINA.

AN INCIDENT IN THE LIFE OF FRANÇOIS BOUCHER.

' On ne badine pas avec l'amour.'

THE scene, a wood.   A shepherd tip-toe creeping,
    Carries a basket, whence a billet peeps,
To lay beside a silk-clad Oread sleeping
    Under an urn ; yet not so sound she sleeps
But that she plainly sees his graceful act ;
' He thinks she thinks he thinks she sleeps,' in fact.

One hardly needs the ' *Peint par François Boucher.*'

    All the sham life comes back again,—one sees

Alcôves, *Ruelles*, the *Lever*, and the *Coucher*,

    Patches and Ruffles, *Roués* and *Marquises;*

The little great, the infinite small thing

That ruled the hour when Louis Quinze was king.

For these were yet the days of halcyon weather,—-

    A Martin's summer when the nation swam,

Aimless and easy as a wayward feather,

    Down the full tide of jest and epigram ;—

A careless time, when France's bluest blood

Beat to the tune of ' After us the flood.'

Plain Roland still was placidly 'inspecting,'

    Not now Camille had stirred the Café Foy ;

Marat was young, and Guillotin dissecting,

    Corday unborn, and Lamballe in Savoie ;

No *faubourg* yet had heard the Tocsin ring :—

This was the summer—when Grasshoppers sing.

And far afield were sun-baked savage creatures,
　　Female and male, that tilled the earth, and wrung
Want from the soil ;—lean things with livid features,
　　Shape of bent man, and voice that never sung :
These were the Ants, for yet to Jacques Bonhomme
Tumbrils were not, nor any sound of drum.

But Boucher was a Grasshopper, and painted,—
　　Rose-water Raphael,—*en couleur de rose,*
The crowned Caprice, whose sceptre, nowise sainted,
　　Swayed the light realm of ballets and bon-mots ;—
Ruled the dim boudoir's *demi-jour,* or drove
Pink-ribboned flocks through some pink-flowered
　　grove.

A laughing Dame, who sailed a laughing cargo
　　Of flippant loves along the *Fleuve du Tendre;*
Whose greatest grace was *jupes à la Camargo,*
　　Whose gentlest merit *gentiment se rendre;*—
Queen of the rouge-cheeked Hours, whose footsteps fell
　　To Rameau's notes, in dances by Gardel—

Her Boucher served, till Nature's self betraying,
  As Wordsworth sings, the heart that loved her not,
Made of his work a land of languid Maying,
  Filled with false gods and muses misbegot ;—
A Versailles Eden of cosmetic youth,
Wherein most things went naked, save the Truth.

Once, only once,—perhaps the last night's revels
  Palled in the after-taste,—our Boucher sighed
For that first beauty, falsely named the Devil's,
  Young-lipped, unlessoned, joyous, and clear-eyed ;
Flung down his palette like a weary man,
And sauntered slowly through the Rue Sainte-Anne.

Wherefore, we know not ; but, at times, far nearer
  Things common come, and lineaments half-seen
Grow in a moment magically clearer ;—
  Perhaps, as he walked, the grass he called 'too green'
Rose and rebuked him, or the earth ' ill-lighted '
Silently smote him with the charms he slighted.

But, as he walked, he tired of god and goddess,
   Nymphs that deny, and shepherds that appeal;
Stale seemed the trick of kerchief and of bodice,
   Folds that confess, and flutters that reveal;
Then as he grew more sad and disenchanted,
Forthwith he spied the very thing he wanted.

So, in the Louvre, the passer-by might spy some
   Arch-looking head, with half-evasive air,
Start from behind the fruitage of Van Huysum,
   Grape-bunch and melon, nectarine and pear :—
Here 'twas no Venus of Batavian city,
But a French girl, young, *piquante*, bright, and pretty.

Graceful she was, as some slim marsh-flower shaken
   Among the sallows, in the breezy Spring;
Blithe as the first blithe song of birds that waken,
   Fresh as a fresh young pear-tree blossoming;
Black was her hair as any blackbird's feather;
Just for her mouth, two rose-buds grew together.

Sloes were her eyes; but her soft cheeks were peaches,

    Hued like an Autumn pippin, where the red

Seems to have burned right through the skin, and

    reaches

    E'en to the core; and if you spoke, it spread

Up till the blush had vanquished all the brown,

And, like two birds, the sudden lids dropped down.

As Boucher smiled, the bright black eyes ceased

    dancing,

    As Boucher spoke, the dainty red eclipse

Filled all the face from cheek to brow, enhancing

    Half a shy smile that dawned around the lips.

Then a shrill mother rose upon the view;

' *Cerises, M'sieu ? Rosine, dépêchez-vous !* '

Deep in the fruit her hands Rosina buries,

    Soon in the scale the ruby bunches lay.

The painter, watching the suspended cherries,

    Never had seen such little fingers play ;—

As for the arm, no Hebè's could be rounder ;

Low in his heart a whisper said ' I 've found her.'

' Woo first the mother, if you 'd win the daughter ! '
   Boucher was charmed, and turned to *Madame Mère,*
Almost with tears of suppliance besought her
   Leave to immortalize a face so fair ;
Praised and cajoled so craftily that straightway
Voici Rosina,—standing at his gateway.

Shy at the first, in time Rosina's laughter
   Rang through the studio as the girlish face
Peeped from some painter's travesty, or after
   Showed like an Omphalè in lion's case ;
Gay as a thrush, that from the morning dew
Pipes to the light its clear ' *Réveillez-vous.*'

Just a mere child with sudden ebullitions,
   Flashes of fun, and little bursts of song,
Petulant pains, and fleeting pale contritions,
   Mute little moods of misery and wrong ;
Only a child, of Nature's rarest making,
Wistful and sweet,—and with a heart for breaking !

Day after day the little loving creature
  Came and returned ; and still the Painter felt,
Day after day, the old theatric Nature
  Fade from his sight, and like a shadow melt,—
Paniers and Powder, Pastoral and Scene,
Killed by the simple beauty of Rosine.

As for the girl, she turned to her new being,—
  Came, as a bird that hears its fellow call ;
Blessed, as the blind that blesses God for seeing ;
  Grew as a flower on which the sun-rays fall ;
Loved if you will ;—she never named it so :
Love comes unseen,—we only see it go.

There is a figure among Boucher's sketches,
  Slim,—a child-face, the eyes as black as beads,
Head set askance, and hand that shyly stretches
  Flowers to the passer, with a look that pleads.
This was no other than Rosina surely ;—
None Boucher knew could else have looked so purely.

But forth her Story, for I will not tarry,—
   Whether he loved the little 'nut-brown maid ;'
If, of a truth, he counted this to carry
   Straight to the end, or just the whim obeyed,
Nothing we know, but only that before
More had been done, a finger tapped the door.

Opened Rosina to the unknown comer.
   'Twas a young girl—' *une pauvre fille,*' she said,
' They had been growing poorer all the summer ;
   Father was lame, and mother lately dead ;
Bread was so dear, and,—oh ! but want was bitter,
Would Monsieur pay to have her for a sitter ?

Men called her pretty.'   Boucher looked a minute :
   Yes, she was pretty ; and her face beside
Shamed her poor clothing by a something in it,—
   Grace, and a presence hard to be denied ;
This was no common offer it was certain ;—
' *Allez,* Rosina ! sit behind the curtain.'

Meantime the Painter, with a mixed emotion,

    Drew and re-drew his ill-disguised Marquise,

Passed in due time from praises to devotion;

    Last when his sitter left him on his knees,

Rose in a maze of passion and surprise,—

Rose, and beheld Rosina's saddened eyes.

Thrice-happy France, whose facile sons inherit

    Still in the old traditionary way,

Power to enjoy—with yet a rarer merit,

    Power to forget.   Our Boucher rose, I say,

With hand still prest to heart, with pulses throbbing,

And blankly stared at poor Rosina sobbing.

'This was no model, *M'sieu*, but a lady.'

    Boucher was silent, for he knew it true.

'*Est-ce que vous l'aimez ?*'   Never answer made he!

    Ah, for the old love fighting with the new!

'*Est-ce que vous l'aimez ?*' sobbed Rosina's sorrow.

'*Bon!*' murmured Boucher; 'she will come to-

    morrow.'

How like a Hunter thou, O Time, dost harry
　　Us, thine oppressed, and pleasured with the chase
Sparest to strike thy sorely-running quarry,
　　Following not less with unrelenting face.
Time, if Love hunt, and Sorrow hunt, with thee,
Woe to the Fawn !　There is no way to flee.

Woe to Rosina !　By To-morrow stricken,
　　Swift from her life the sun of gold declined.
Nothing remained but those gray shades that thicken,
　　Cloud and the cold,—the loneliness—the wind.
Only a little by the door she lingers,—
Waits, with wrung lip and interwoven fingers.

No, not a sign.　Already with the Painter
　　Grace and the nymphs began recovered reign ;
Truth was no more, and Nature, waxing fainter,
　　Paled to the old sick Artifice again.
Seeing Rosina going out to die,
How should he know what Fame had passed him by ?

Going to die ! For who shall waste in sadness,

  Shorn of the sun, the very warmth and light,

Miss the green welcome of the sweet earth's gladness,

  Lose the round life that only Love makes bright :

There is no succour if these things are taken.

None but Death loves the lips by Love forsaken.

So, in a little, when those Two had parted,—

  Tired of himself, and weary as before,

Boucher remembering, sick and sorry-hearted,

  Stayed for a moment by Rosina's door.

'Ah, the poor child !' the neighbours cry of her,

' *Morte, M'sieu, morte !   On dit,—des peines du cœur.*'

Just for a second, say, the tidings shocked him,

  Say, in his eye a sudden tear-drop shone,—

Just for a second a dull feeling mocked him

  With a vague sense of something priceless gone ;

Then,—for at best 'twas but the empty type,

The husk of man with which the days were ripe,—

Then, he forgot her. But, for you that slew her,
  You, her own sister, that with airy ease,
Just for a moment's fancy could undo her,
  Pass on your way.   A little while, Marquise,
Be the sky silent, be the sea serene ;
A pleasant passage—*à Sainte Guillotine.*

As for Rosina,—for the quiet sleeper,
  Whether stone hides her, or the happy grass,
If the sun quickens, if the dews beweep her,
  Laid in the Madeleine or Montparnasse,
Nothing we know,—but that her heart is cold,
Poor beating heart !   And so the story 's told.

A REVOLUTIONARY RELIC.

I.

OLD it is, and worn and battered,
    As I lift it from the stall ;
And the leaves are frayed and tattered,
And the pendent sides are shattered,
    Pierced and blackened by a ball.

II.

'Tis the tale of grief and gladness
    Told by sad St. Pierre of yore,
That in front of France's madness
Hangs a strange seductive sadness,
    Grown pathetic evermore.

III.

And a perfume round it hovers,

  Which the pages half reveal,

For a folded corner covers,

Interlaced, two names of lovers,—

  A ' Savignac' and ' Lucile.'

IV.

As I read I marvel whether,

  In some pleasant old château,

Once they read this book together,

In the scented summer weather,

  With the shining Loire below ?

V.

Nooked—secluded from espial,

  Did Love slip and snare them so,

While the hours danced round the dial

To the sound of flute and viol,

  In that pleasant old château ?

VI.

Did it happen that no single

    Word of mouth could either speak ?

Did the brown and gold hair mingle,

Did the shamed skin thrill and tingle

    To the shock of cheek and cheek ?

VII.

Did they feel with that first flushing

    Some new sudden power to feel,

Some new inner spring set gushing

At the names together rushing

    Of ' Savignac ' and ' Lucile ' ?

VIII.

Did he drop on knee before her—

    ' *Son Amour, son Cœur, sa Reine* '—

In his high-flown way, adore her,

Urgent, eloquent implore her,

    Plead his pleasure and his pain ?

D

IX.

Did she turn with sight swift-dimming,

And the quivering lip we know,

With the full, slow eyelid brimming,

With the languorous pupil swimming,

Like the love of Mirabeau ?

X.

Stretch her hand from cloudy frilling,

For his eager lips to press ;

In a flash all fate fulfilling

Did he catch her, trembling, thrilling—

Crushing life to one caress ?

XI.

Did they sit in that dim sweetness

Of attained love's after-calm,

Marking not the world—its meetness,

Marking Time not, nor his fleetness,

Only happy, palm to palm ?

XII.

Till at last she,—sunlight smiting

  Red on wrist and cheek and hair,—

Sought the page where love first lighting,

Fixed their fate, and, in this writing,

  Fixed the record of it there.

      *   *   *

XIII.

Did they marry midst the smother,

  Shame and slaughter of it all ?

Did she wander like that other

Woful, wistful, wife and mother,

  Round and round his prison wall ;—

XIV.

Wander wailing, as the plover

  Waileth, wheeleth, desolate,

Heedless of the hawk above her,

While as yet the rushes cover,

  Waning fast, her wounded mate ;—

XV.

Wander, till his love's eyes met hers,

    Fixed and wide in their despair?

Did he burst his prison fetters,

Did he write sweet, yearning letters,

    '*A Lucile,—en Angleterre*'?

XVI.

Letters where the reader, reading,

    Halts him with a sudden stop,

For he feels a man's heart bleeding,

Draining out its pain's exceeding—

    Half a life, at every drop :

XVII.

Letters where Love's iteration

    Seems to warble and to rave ;

Letters where the pent sensation

Leaps to lyric exultation,

    Like a song-bird from a grave.

XVIII.

Where, through Passion's wild repeating

    Peeps the Pagan and the Gaul,

Politics and love competing,

Abelard and Cato greeting,

    Rousseau ramping over all. ˙

XIX.

Yet your critic's right—you waive it,

    Whirled along the fever-flood ;

And its touch of truth shall save it,

And its tender rain shall lave it,

For at least you read *Amavit,*

    Written there in tears of blood.

     *   *   *

XX.

Did they hunt him to his hiding,

    Tracking traces in the snow ?

Did they tempt him out, confiding,

Shoot him ruthless down, deriding,

    By the ruined old château ?

XXI.

Left to lie, with thin lips resting

Frozen to a smile of scorn,

Just the bitter thought's suggesting,

At this excellent new jesting

Of the rabble Devil-born.

XXII.

Till some ' tiger-monkey,' finding

These few words the covers bear,

Some swift rush of pity blinding,

Sent them in the shot-pierced binding

' A Lucile, en Angleterre.'

*　　　　*　　　　*

XXIII.

Fancies only !   Nought the covers,

Nothing more the leaves reveal,

Yet I love it for its lovers,

For the dream that round it hovers

Of ' Savignac ' and ' Lucile.'

BEFORE SEDAN.

' The dead hand clasped a letter.'

SPECIAL CORRESPONDENCE.

HERE, in this leafy place,

    Quiet he lies,

Cold, with his sightless face

    Turned to the skies ;

'Tis but another dead ;

All you can say is said.

Carry his body hence,—
    Kings must have slaves ;
Kings climb to eminence
    Over men's graves :
So this man's eye is dim ;—
Throw the earth over him.

What was the white you touched,
    There, at his side ?
Paper his hand had clutched
    Tight ere he died ;—
Message or wish, may be ;—
Smooth the folds out and see.

Hardly the worst of us
    Here could have smiled !—
Only the tremulous
    Words of a child ;—
Prattle, that has for stops
Just a few ruddy drops.

Look.   She is sad to miss,

    Morning and night,

His—her dead father's—kiss ;

    Tries to be bright,

Good to mamma, and sweet.

That is all.   ' Marguerite.'

Ah, if beside the dead

    Slumbered the pain !

Ah, if the hearts that bled

    Slept with the slain !

If the grief died ;—But no ;—

Death will not have it so.

AVICE.

' On serait tenté de lui dire, Bonjour, Mademoiselle la Bergeronnette.'—VICTOR HUGO.

I.

THOUGH the voice of modern schools

Has demurred,

By the dreamy Asian creed

'Tis averred,

That the souls of men, released

From their bodies when deceased,

Sometimes enter in a beast,—

Or a bird.

II.

I have watched you long, Avice,—

Watched you so,

I have found your secret out ;

And I know

That the restless ribboned things,

Where your slope of shoulder springs,

Are but undeveloped wings

That will grow.

III.

When you enter in a room,

It is stirred

With the wayward, flashing flight

Of a bird ;

And you speak—and bring with you

Leaf and sun-ray, bud and blue,

And the wind-breath and the dew

At a word.

IV.

When you called to me my name,

Then again

When I heard your single cry

In the lane,

All the sound was as the 'sweet'

Which the birds to birds repeat

In their thank-song to the heat

After rain.

V.

When you sang the *Schwalbenlied*,

'Twas absurd,—

But it seemed no human note

That I heard ;

For your strain had all the trills,

All the little shakes and stills,

Of the over-song that rills

From a bird.

VI.

You have just their eager, quick

'*Airs de tête,*'

All their flush and fever-heat

When elate ;

Every bird-like nod and beck,

And a bird's own curve of neck

When she gives a little peck

To her mate.

VII.

When you left me, only now,

In that furred,

Puffed, and feathered Polish dress,

I was spurred

Just to catch you, O my Sweet,

By the bodice trim and neat,—

Just to feel your heart a-beat,

Like a bird.

VIII.

Yet, alas ! Love's light you deign

But to wear

As the dew upon your plumes,

And you care

Not a whit for rest or hush ;

But the leaves, the lyric gush,

And the wing-power, and the rush

Of the air.

IX.

So I dare not woo you, Sweet,

For a day,

Lest I lose you in a flash,

As I may ;

Did I tell you tender things,

You would shake your sudden wings ;—

You would start from him who sings,

And away.

A DIALOGUE FROM PLATO.

' *Le temps le mieux employé est celui qu'on perd.*'
CLAUDE TILLIER.

I 'D ' read' three hours.   Both notes and text
    Were fast a mist becoming ;
In bounced a vagrant bee, perplexed,
    And filled the room with humming;

Then out.   The casement's leafage sways,
    And, parted light, discloses
Miss Di., with hat and book,—a maze
    Of muslin mixed with roses.

'You're reading Greek?' 'I am—and you?'

'O, mine's a mere romancer!'

'So Plato is.'   'Then read him—do;

And I'll read mine in answer.'

I read.   'My Plato (Plato, too,—

That wisdom thus should harden!)

Declares "blue eyes look doubly blue

Beneath a Dolly Varden."'

She smiled.   'My book in turn avers

(No author's name is stated)

That sometimes those Philosophers

Are sadly mis-translated.'

'But hear,—the next's in stronger style:

The Cynic School asserted

That two red lips which part and smile

May not be controverted!'

She smiled once more—'My book, I find,
  Observes some modern doctors
Would make the Cynics out a kind
  Of album-verse concoctors.'

Then I—'Why not? "Ephesian law,
  No less than time's tradition,
Enjoined fair speech on all who saw
  DIANA's apparition."'

She blushed—this time. 'If Plato's page
  No wiser precept teaches,
Then I'd renounce that doubtful sage,
  And walk to Burnham-beeches.'

'Agreed,' I said. 'For Socrates
  (I find he too is talking)
Thinks Learning can't remain at ease
  While Beauty goes a-walking.'

E

She read no more.   I leapt the sill:

The sequel's scarce essential—

Nay, more than this, I hold it still

Profoundly confidential.

AN AUTUMN IDYLL.

' Sweet Themmes ! runne softly, till I end my song.'—SPENSER.

LAWRENCE.   FRANK.   JACK.

LAWRENCE.

HERE, where the beech-nuts drop among the grasses,

   Push the boat in, and throw the rope ashore.

Jack, hand me out the claret and the glasses;

   Here let us sit.   We landed here before.

FRANK.

Jack's undecided.   Say, *formose puer*,

   Bent in a dream above the ' water wan,'

Shall we row higher, for the reeds are fewer,

   There by the pollards, where you see the swan ?

JACK.

Hist ! That's a pike. Look—nose against the river,

Gaunt as a wolf,—the sly old privateer !

Enter a gudgeon. Snap,—a gulp, a shiver ;—

Exit the gudgeon. Let us anchor here.

FRANK (*in the grass*).

Jove, what a day ! Black Care upon the crupper

Nods at his post, and slumbers in the sun ;

Half of Theocritus, with a touch of Tupper,

Churns in my head. The frenzy has begun !

LAWRENCE.

Sing to us then. Damœtas in a choker,

Much out of tune, will edify the rooks.

FRANK.

Sing you again. So musical a croaker

Surely will draw the fish upon the hooks.

JACK.

Sing while you may.   The beard of manhood still is

    Faint on your cheeks, but I, alas ! am old.

Doubtless you yet believe in Amaryllis ;—

    Sing me of Her, whose name may not be told.

FRANK.

Listen, O Thames !   His budding beard is riper,

    Say—by a week.   Well, Lawrence, shall we sing ?

LAWRENCE.

Yes, if you will.   But ere I play the piper,

    Let him declare the prize he has to bring.

JACK.

Hear then, my Shepherds.   Lo, to him accounted

    First in the song, a Pipe I will impart ;—

This, my Belovèd, marvellously mounted,

    Amber and foam,—a miracle of art.

LAWRENCE.

Lordly the gift.   O Muse of many numbers

  Grant me a soft alliterative song !

FRANK.

Me too, O Muse!   And when the Umpire slumbers,

  Sting him with gnats a summer evening long.

LAWRENCE.

Not in a cot, begarlanded of spiders,

  Not where the brook traditionally purls,—

No, in the Row, supreme among the riders,

  Seek I the gem,—the paragon of girls.

FRANK.

Not in the waste of column and of coping,

  Not in the sham and stucco of a square,—

No, on a June-lawn, to the water sloping,

  Stands she I honour, beautifully fair.

LAWRENCE.

Dark-haired is mine, with splendid tresses plaited

    Back from the brows, imperially curled ;

Calm as a grand, far-looking Caryatid,

    Holding the roof that covers in a world.

FRANK.

Dark-haired is mine, with breezy ripples swinging

    Loose as a vine-branch blowing in the morn ;

Eyes like the morning, mouth for ever singing,

    Blithe as a bird, new risen from the corn.

LAWRENCE.

Best is the song with music interwoven :

    Mine 's a musician,—musical at heart,—

Throbs to the gathered grieving of Beethoven,

    Sways to the light coquetting of Mozart.

FRANK.

Best? You should hear mine trilling out a ballad,

　Queen at a pic-nic, leader of the glees,

Not too divine to toss you up a salad,

　Great in Sir Roger danced among the trees.

LAWRENCE.

Ah, when the thick night flares with dropping torches,

　Ah, when the crush-room empties of the swarm,

Pleasant the hand that, in the gusty porches,

　Light as a snow-flake, settles on your arm.

FRANK.

Better the twilight and the cheery chatting,—

　Better the dim, forgotten garden-seat,

Where one may lie, and watch the fingers tatting,

　Lounging with Bran or Bevis at her feet.

LAWRENCE.

All worship mine.   Her purity doth hedge her
  Round with so delicate divinity, that men,
Stained to the soul with money-bag and ledger,
  Bend to the goddess, manifest again.

FRANK.

None worship mine.   But some, I fancy, love her,—
  Cynics to boot.   I know the children run,
Seeing her come, for naught that I discover,
  Save that she brings the summer and the sun.

LAWRENCE.

Mine is a Lady, beautiful and queenly,
  Crowned with a sweet, continual control,
Grandly forbearing, lifting life serenely
  E'en to her own nobility of soul.

FRANK.

Mine is a Woman, kindly beyond measure,

    Fearless in praising, faltering in blame ;

Simply devoted to other people's pleasure,—

    Jack's sister Florence,—now you know her name.

LAWRENCE.

'Jack's sister Florence !' Never, Francis, never.

    Jack, do you hear? Why, it was she I meant.

She like the country ! Ah, she's far too clever—

FRANK.

There you are wrong. I know her down in Kent.

LAWRENCE.

You'll get a sunstroke, standing with your head bare.

    Sorry to differ. Jack,—the word's with you.

FRANK.

How is it, Umpire? Though the motto's threadbare,

'*Cælum, non animum*'—is, I take it, true.

JACK.

'*Souvent femme varie*,' as a rule, is truer;

Flattered, I'm sure,—but both of you romance.

Happy to further suit of either wooer,

Merely observing—you haven't got a chance.

LAWRENCE.

Yes.   But the Pipe—

FRANK.

The Pipe is what we care for,—

JACK.

Well, in this case, I scarcely need explain,

Judgment of mine were indiscreet, and therefore,—

Peace to you both.   The Pipe I shall retain.

A GARDEN IDYLL.

A LADY.   A POET.

THE LADY.

I.

SIR POET, ere you crossed the lawn

  (If it was wrong to watch you, pardon),

Behind this weeping birch withdrawn,

  I watched you saunter round the garden.

I saw you bend beside the phlox,

  Pluck, as you passed, a sprig of myrtle,

Review my well-ranged hollyhocks,

  Smile at the fountain's slender spurtle;

II.

You paused beneath the cherry-tree,

    Where my marauder thrush was singing,

Peered at the bee-hives curiously,

    And narrowly escaped a stinging ;

And then—you see I watched—you passed

    Down the espalier walk that reaches

Out to the western wall, and last

    Dropped on the seat before the peaches.

III.

What was your thought? You waited long.

    Sublime or graceful,—grave,—satiric ?

A Morris Greek-and-Gothic song ?

    A tender Tennysonian lyric ?

Tell me. That garden-seat shall be,

    So long as speech renown disperses,

Illustrious as the spot where he—

    The gifted Blank—composed his verses.

THE POET.

IV.

Madam,—whose uncensorious eye

 Grows gracious over certain pages,

Wherein the Jester's maxims lie,

 It may be, thicker than the Sage's—

I hear but to obey, and could

 Mere wish of mine the pleasure do you,

Some verse as whimsical as Hood,—

 As gay as Praed,—should answer to you.

V.

But, though the common voice proclaims

 Our only serious vocation

Confined to giving nothings names,

 And dreams a 'local habitation;'

Believe me, there are tuneless days,

 When neither marble, brass, nor vellum,

Would profit much by any lays

 That haunt the poet's cerebellum.

VI.

More empty things, I fear, than rhymes,
    More idle things than songs, absorb it;
The 'finely-frenzied' eye, at times,
    Reposes mildly in its orbit;
And, painful truth, at times, to him,
    Whose jog-trot thought is nowise restive,
'A primrose by a river's brim'
    Is absolutely unsuggestive.

VII.

The fickle Muse! As ladies will,
    She sometimes wearies of her wooer;
A goddess, yet a woman still,
    She flies the more that we pursue her;
In short, with worst as well as best,
    Five months in six, your hapless poet
Is just as prosy as the rest,
    But cannot comfortably show it.

VIII.

You thought, no doubt, the garden-scent
   Brings back some brief-winged bright sensation
Of love that came and love that went,—
   Some fragrance of a lost flirtation,
Born when the cuckoo changes song,
   Dead ere the apple's red is on it,
That should have been an epic long,
   Yet scarcely served to fill a sonnet.

IX.

Or else you thought,—the murmuring noon,
   He turns it to a lyric sweeter,
With birds that gossip in the tune,
   And windy bough-swing in the metre;
Or else the zigzag fruit-tree arms
   Recall some dream of harp-prest bosoms,
Round singing mouths, and chanted charms,
   And mediæval orchard blossoms,—

X.

Quite *à la mode.*   Alas for prose,—

   My vagrant fancies only rambled

Back to the red-walled Rectory close,

   Where first my graceless boyhood gamboled,

Climbed on the dial, teased the fish,

   And chased the kitten round the beeches,

Till widening instincts made me wish

   For certain slowly-ripening peaches.

XI.

Three peaches.   Not the Graces three

   Had more equality of beauty :

I would not look, yet went to see ;

   I wrestled with Desire and Duty ;

I felt the pangs of those who feel

   The Laws of Property beset them ;

The conflict made my reason reel,

   And, half-abstractedly, I ate them ;—

F

XII.

Or Two of them.   Forthwith Despair—

   More keen that one of these was rotten—

Moved me to seek some forest lair

   Where I might hide and dwell forgotten,

Attired in skins, by berries stained,

   Absolved from brushes and ablution ;—

But, ere my sylvan haunt was gained,

   Fate gave me up to execution.

XIII.

I saw it all but now.   The grin

   That gnarled old Gardener Sandy's features ;

. My father, scholar-like and thin,

   Unroused, the tenderest of creatures ;

I saw—ah me—I saw again

   My dear and deprecating mother ;

And then, remembering the cane,

   Regretted—that I 'd left the other.

TU QUOQUE.

AN IDYLL IN THE CONSERVATORY.

' —romprons-nous,
Ou ne romprons-nous pas ?'
LE DÉPIT AMOUREUX.

NELLIE.

IF I were you, when ladies at the play, sir,

    Beckon and nod, a melodrama through,

I would not turn abstractedly away, sir,

    If I were you !

FRANK.

If I were you, when persons I affected,

    Wait for three hours to take me down to Kew,

I would, at least, pretend I recollected,

    If I were you !

NELLIE.

If I were you, when ladies are so lavish,

    Sir, as to keep me every waltz but two,

I would not dance with *odious* Miss M'Tavish,

    If I were you!

FRANK.

If I were you, who vow you cannot suffer

    Whiff of the best,—the mildest ' honey-dew,'

I would not dance with smoke-consuming Puffer,

    If I were you!

NELLIE.

If I were you, I would not, sir, be bitter,

    Even to write the ' Cynical Review ; '—

FRANK.

No, I should doubtless find flirtation fitter,

    If I were you!

NELLIE.

Really! You would? Why, Frank, you're quite
    delightful,—
Hot as Othello, and as black of hue ; .
Borrow my fan. I would not look so *frightful,*
    If I were you!

FRANK.

'It is the cause.' I mean your chaperon is
    Bringing some well-curled juvenile. Adieu !
I shall retire. I'd spare that poor Adonis, .
    If I were you!

NELLIE.

Go, if you will. At once ! And by express, sir !
    Where shall it be? To China—or Peru?
Go. I should leave inquirers my address, sir,
    If I were you!

FRANK.

No,—I remain.   To stay and fight a duel
  Seems, on the whole, the proper thing to do—
Ah, you are strong,—I would not then be cruel,
  If I were you !

NELLIE.

One does not like one's feelings to be doubted,—

FRANK.

One does not like one's friends to misconstrue,—

NELLIE.

If I confess that I a wee-bit pouted ?—

FRANK.

I should admit that I was *piqué*, too.

NELLIE.

Ask me to dance.   I 'd say no more about it,
  If I were you !

[Waltz—*Exeunt.*]

'LE ROMAN DE LA ROSE.'

POOR Rose ! I lift you from the street—
    Far better I should own you
Than you should lie for random feet
    Where careless hands have thrown you.

Poor pinky petals, crushed and torn !
    Did heartless Mayfair use you,
Then cast you forth to lie forlorn,
    For chariot-wheels to bruise you ?

I saw you last in Edith's hair.

Rose, you would scarce discover

That I she passed upon the stair

Was Edith's favoured lover,

A month—'a little month '—ago—

O theme for moral writer !—

'Twixt you and me, my Rose, you know,

She might have been politer;

But let that pass.   She gave you then—

Behind the oleander—

To one, perhaps, of all the men,

Who best could understand her,—

Cyril, that, duly flattered, took,

As only Cyril's able,

With just the same Arcadian look

He used, last night, for Mabel;

Then, having waltzed till every star

    Had paled away in morning,

Lit up his cynical cigar,

    And tossed you downward, scorning.

Kismet, my Rose ! Revenge is sweet,—

    She made my heart-strings quiver ;

And yet—You shan't lie in the street

    I 'll drop you in the River.

AD ROSAM.

' Mitte sectari ROSA *quo locorum*
Sera moretur.'

HOR. I. 38.

I.

I HAD a vacant dwelling—

    Where situated, I,

As nought can serve the telling,

    Decline to specify ;—

Enough 'twas neither haunted,

    Entailed, nor out of date ;

I put up ' Tenant Wanted,'

    And left the rest to Fate.

II.

Then, Rose, you passed the window,—

   I see you passing yet,—

Ah, what could I within do,

   When, Rose, our glances met!

You snared me, Rose, with ribbons,

   Your rose-mouth made me thrall,

Brief—briefer far than Gibbon's,

   Was my ' Decline and Fall.'

III.

I heard the summons spoken

   That all hear—king and clown :

You smiled—the ice was broken ;

   You stopped—the bill was down.

How blind we are !   It never

   Occurred to me to seek

If you had come for ever,

   Or only for a week.

IV.

The words your voice neglected,

   Seemed written in your eyes ;

The thought your heart protected,

   Your cheek told, missal-wise ;—

I read the rubric plainly

   As any Expert could ;

In short, we dreamed,—insanely,

   As only lovers should.

V.

I broke the tall Œnone,

   That then my chambers graced,

Because she seemed ' too bony,'

   To suit your purist taste ;

And you, without vexation,

   May certainly confess

Some graceful approbation,

   Designed *à mon adresse.*

VI.

You liked me then, *carina*,—
　　You liked me then, I think ;
For your sake gall had been a
　　Mere tonic-cup to drink ;
For your sake, bonds were trivial,
　　The rack, a *tour-de-force;*
And banishment, convivial,—
　　You coming too, of course.

VII.

Then, Rose, a word in jest meant
　　Would throw you in a state
That no well-timed investment
　　Could quite alleviate ;
Beyond a Paris trousseau
　　You prized my smile, I know,
I, yours—ah, more than Rousseau
　　The lip of d' Houdetot.

VIII.

Then, Rose,—But why pursue it ?

When Fate begins to frown

Best write the final '*fuit,*'

And gulp the physic down.

And yet,—and yet, that only,

The song should end with this :—

You left me,—left me lonely,

Rosa mutabilis !

IX.

Left me, with Time for Mentor,

(A dreary *tête-à-tête !*)

To pen my ' Last Lament,' or

Extemporize to Fate,

In blankest verse disclosing

My bitterness of mind,—

Which is, I learn, composing

In cases of the kind.

X.

No, Rose.   Though you refuse me,

Culture the pang prevents ;

' I am not made '—excuse me—

' Of so slight elements ; '

I leave to common lovers

The hemlock or the hood ;

My rarer soul recovers

In dreams of public good.

XI.

The Roses of this nation—

Or so I understand

From careful computation—

Exceed the gross demand ;

And, therefore, in civility

To maids that can't be matched,

No man of sensibility

Should linger unattached.

XII.

So, without further fashion—

A modern Curtius,

Plunging, from pure compassion,

To aid the overplus,—

I sit down, sad—not daunted,

And, in my weeds, begin

A new card—' Tenant Wanted ;

Particulars within.'

THE LOVE-LETTER.

' J'ai vu les mœurs de mon temps, et j'ai publié cette lettre.'
LA NOUVELLE HÉLOISE.

IF this should fail, why then I scarcely know

    What could succeed.   Here's brilliancy (and

        banter),

Byron *ad lib.*, a chapter of Rousseau ;—

    If this should fail, then *tempora mutantur ;*

Style's out of date, and love, as a profession,

Acquires no aid from beauty of expression.

G

'The men who think as I, I fear, are few,'

    (Cynics would say 'twere well if they were fewer) ;

'I am not what I seem, '—(indeed, 'tis true ;

    Though, as a sentiment, it might be newer) ;

'Mine is a soul whose deeper feelings lie

More deep than words '—(as these exemplify).

'I will not say when first your beauty's sun

    Illumed my life,'—(it needs imagination) ;

'For me to see you and to love were one,'—

    (This will account for some precipitation) ;

'Let it suffice that worship more devoted

Ne'er throbbed,' *et cætera.*   The rest is quoted.

'If Love can look with all-prophetic eye,'—

    (Ah, if he could, how many would be single!),

'If truly spirit unto spirit cry,'—

    (The ears of some most terribly must tingle !)

' Then I have dreamed you will not turn your face.'

This next, I think, is more than commonplace.

'Why should we speak, if Love, interpreting,

   Forestall the speech with favour found before?

Why should we plead?—it were an idle thing,

   If Love himself be Love's ambassador !'

Blot, as I live.   Shall we erase it?   No ;—

'Twill show we write *currente calamo.*

' My fate,—my fortune, I commit to you,—

   (In point of fact, the latter 's not extensive) ;

' Without you I am poor indeed,'—(strike through,

   'Tis true but crude—'twould make her apprehen-

     sive) ;

' My life is yours—I lay it at your feet,'

(Having no choice but Hymen or the Fleet).

'Give me the right to stand within the shrine,

    Where never yet my faltering feet intruded ;

Give me the right to call you wholly mine,'—

    (That is, Consols and Three per Cents included) ;

'To guard your rest from every care that cankers,—

To keep your life,'—(and balance at your banker's).

'Compel me not to long for your reply ;

    Suspense makes havoc with the mind'—(and

        muscles) ;

'Winged Hope takes flight,'—(which means that I

        must fly,·

    Default of funds, to Paris or to Brussels) ;

'I cannot wait ! My own, my queen—Priscilla !

Write by return.' And *now* for a Manila !

'Miss Blank,' at 'Blank.' Jemima, let it go,

    And I, meanwhile, will idle with 'Sir Walter ; '

Stay, let me keep the first rough copy, though —

  'Twill serve again.   There's but the name to alter,

And Love, that needs, must knock at every portal,

In formâ pauperis.   We are but mortal !

A VIRTUOSO.

I.

Be seated, pray. 'A grave appeal'?
    The sufferers by the war, of course ;
Ah, what a sight for us who feel,—
    This monstrous *mélodrame* of Force !
We, Sir, we connoisseurs, should know,
    On whom its heaviest burden falls ;
Collections shattered at a blow,
    Museums turned to hospitals !

II.

'And worse,' you say ; 'the wide distress !'
 Alas, 'tis true distress exists,
Though, let me add, our worthy Press
 Have no mean skill as colourists ;—
Speaking of colour, next your seat
 There hangs a sketch from Vernet's hand ;
Some Moscow fancy, incomplete,
 Yet not indifferently planned ;

III.

Note specially the gray old Guard,
 Who tears his tattered coat to wrap
A closer bandage round the scarred
 And frozen comrade in his lap ;—
But, as regards the present war,—
 Now don't you think our pride of pence
Goes—may I say it ?—somewhat far
 For objects of benevolence ?

IV.

You hesitate.   For my part, I—

 Though ranking Paris next to Rome,

Æsthetically—still reply ·

 That 'Charity begins at Home.'

The words remind me.   Did you catch

 My so-named 'Hunt'?   The girl's a gem ;

And look how those lean rascals snatch

 The pile of scraps she brings to them !

v.

'But your appeal's for home,' you say,

 For home, and English poor !   Indeed !

I thought Philanthropy to-day

 Was blind to mere domestic need—

However sore—Yet though one grants

 That home should have the foremost claims,

At least these Continental wants

 Assume intelligible names ;

VI.

While here with us—Ah ! who could hope
To verify the varied pleas,
Or from his private means to cope
With all our shrill necessities !
Impossible !   One might as well
Attempt comparison of creeds ;
Or fill that huge Malayan shell
With these half-dozen Indian beads.

VII.

Moreover, add that every one
So well exalts his pet distress,
'Tis—Give to all, or give to none,
If you 'd avoid invidiousness.
Your case, I feel, is sad as A.'s,
The same applies to B.'s and C.'s ;
By my selection I should raise
An alphabet of rivalries ;

VIII.

And life is short,—I see you look

At yonder dish, a priceless bit;

You 'll find it etched in Jacquemart's book,

They say that Raphael painted it ;—

And life is short, you understand ;

So, if I only hold you out

An open though an empty hand,

Why, you 'll forgive me, I 've no doubt.

IX.

Nay, do not rise.   You seem amused ;

One can but be consistent, Sir !

'Twas on these grounds I just refused

Some gushing lady-almoner,—

Believe me, on these very grounds.

Good-bye, then.   Ah, a rarity !

That cost me quite three hundred pounds,—

That Dürer figure,—'Charity.'

LAISSEZ FAIRE.

' Prophete rechts, Prophete links,
Das Weltkind in der Mitten.'
GOETHE'S *Diné zu Coblenz.*

To left, here's B., half-Communist,

Who talks a chastened treason,

And C., a something-else in *ist,*

Harangues, to right, on Reason.

B., from his ' tribune,' fulminates

At Throne and Constitution,

Nay, with the walnuts, advocates

Reform by revolution

While C.'s peculiar coterie

    Have now in full rehearsal

Some patent new Philosophy

    To make doubt universal.

And yet—why not? If zealots burn,

    Their zeal has not affected

My taste for salmon and Sauterne,

    Or I might have objected :—

Friend B., the argument you choose

    Has been by France refuted ;

And C., *mon cher*, your novel views

    Are just Tom Paine, diluted ;

There's but one creed,—that's *Laissez faire ;*

    Behold its mild apostle !

My dear, declamatory pair,

    Although you shout and jostle,

Not your ephemeral hands, nor mine,

Times' Gordian knots shall sunder,—

Will. laid three casks of this old wine :

Who 'll drink the last, I wonder ?

A LEGACY.

Ah, Postumus, we all must go :

    This keen North-Easter nips my shoulder ;

My strength begins to fail ; I know

    You find me older ;

I 've made my Will.   Dear, faithful friend—

    My Muse's friend and not my purse's !

Who still would hear and still commend

    My tedious verses,

How will you live—of these deprived ?

   I 've learned your candid soul.   The venal,—

The sordid friend had scarce survived

   A test so penal ;

But you—Nay, nay, 'tis so.   The rest

   Are not as you : you hide your merit ;

You, more than all, deserve the best

   True friends inherit ;—

Not gold—that hearts like yours despise ;

   Not ' spacious dirt ' (your own expression),

No ; but the rarer, dearer prize—

   The life's confession !

You catch my thought?   What?   Can't you guess ?

   You, you alone, admired my Cantos ;—

I 've left you, P., my whole MS.,

   In three portmanteaus !

TO Q. H. F.

SUGGESTED BY A CHAPTER IN THEODORE MAR'
'HORACE,'

('ANCIENT CLASSICS FOR ENGLISH READERS.')

I.

' HORATIUS FLACCUS, B.C. 8,'

There 's not a doubt about the date,—

    You 're dead and buried :

As you remarked, the seasons roll ;

And 'cross the Styx full many a soul

    Has Charon ferried,

Since, mourned of men and Muses nine,

They laid you on the Esquiline.

II.

And that was centuries ago !

You 'd think we 'd learned enough, I know,

To help refine us,

Since last you trod the Sacred Street,

And tacked from mortal fear to meet

The bore Crispinus ;

Or, by your cold Digentia, set   ·

The web of winter birding-net.

III.

Ours is so far-advanced an age !

Sensation tales, a classic stage,

Commodious villas !

We boast high art, an Albert Hall,

Australian meats, and men who call

Their sires gorillas!

We have a thousand things, you see,

Not dreamt in your philosophy.

IV.

And yet, how strange! Our 'world,' to-day,

Tried in the scale, would scarce outweigh

Your Roman cronies;

Walk in the Park—you'll seldom fail

To find a Sybaris on the rail

By Lydia's ponies,

Or hap on Barrus, wigged and stayed,

Ogling some unsuspecting maid.

V.

The great Gargilius, then, behold!

His 'long-bow' hunting tales of old

Are now but duller;

Fair Neobule too! Is not

One Hebrus here—from Aldershot?

Aha, you colour!

Be wise. There old Canidia sits;

No doubt she's tearing you to bits.

VI.

And look, dyspeptic, brave, and kind,

Comes dear Mæcenas, half behind

      Terentia's skirting ;

Here 's Pyrrha, 'golden-haired' at will ;

Prig Damasippus, preaching still ;

      Asterie flirting,—

Radiant, of course.　We 'll make her black,—

Ask her when Gyges' ship comes back.

VII.

So with the rest.　Who will may trace

Behind the new each elder face

      Defined as clearly ;

Science proceeds, and man stands still ;

Our 'world' to-day 's as good or ill,—

      As cultured (nearly),

As yours was, Horace !　You alone,

Unmatched, unmet, we have not known.

A GAGE D'AMOUR.

(HORACE, III. 8.)

' *Martiis cælebs quid agam Kalendis,*
     ——miraris ?'

I.

CHARLES,—for it seems you wish to know,—

You wonder what could scare me so,

And why, in this long-locked bureau,

          With trembling fingers,—

With tragic air, I now replace

This ancient web of yellow lace,

Among whose faded folds the trace

          Of perfume lingers.

II.

Friend of my youth, severe as true,

I guess the train your thoughts pursue ;

But this my state is nowise due

    To indigestion ;

I had forgotten it was there,

A scarf that Some-one used to wear.

Hinc illæ lachrimæ,—so spare

    Your cynic question.

III.

Some-one who is not girlish now,

And wed long since.   We meet and bow ;

I don't suppose our broken vow

    Affects us keenly ;

Yet, trifling though my act appears, .

Your Sternes would make it ground for tears ;—

One can't disturb the dust of years,

    And smile serenely.

IV.

' My golden locks' are gray and chill,

For hers,—let them be sacred still ;

But yet, I own, a boyish thrill

      Went dancing through me,

Charles, when I held yon yellow lace ;

For, from its dusty hiding-place,

Peeped out an arch, ingenuous face

      That beckoned to me.

V.

We shut our heart up, now-a-days,

Like some old music-box that plays

Unfashionable airs that raise

      Derisive pity ;

Alas,—a nothing starts the spring ;

And lo, the sentimental thing

At once commences quavering

      Its lover's ditty.

VI.

Laugh, if you like.   The boy in me,—

The boy that was,—revived to see

The fresh young smile that shone when she,

     Of old, was tender.

Once more we trod the Golden Way,—

That mother you saw yesterday,

And I, whom none can well portray

     As young, or slender.

VII.

She twirled the flimsy scarf about

Her pretty head, and stepping out,

Slipped arm in mine, with half a pout

     Of childish pleasure.

Where we were bound no mortal knows,

For then you plunged in Ireland's woes,

And brought me blankly back to prose

     And Gladstone's measure.

VIII.

Well, well, the wisest bend to Fate.

My brown old books around me wait,

My pipe still holds, unconfiscate,

  Its wonted station.

Pass me the wine. To Those that keep

The bachelor's secluded sleep

Peaceful, inviolate, and deep,

  I pour libation.

OUTWARD BOUND.

(HORACE, III. 7.)

' Quid fles, Asterie, quem tibi candidi
Primo restituent vere Favonii—
Gygen ? '

I.

COME, Laura, patience.   Time and spring

Your absent Arthur back shall bring,

Enriched with many an Indian thing,

Once more to woo you ;

Him, neither wind nor wave can check

Who, cramped beneath the ' Simla's ' deck,

Still constant, though with stiffened neck,

Makes verses to you.

II.

Would it were wave and wind alone !
The terrors of the torrid zone,
The indiscriminate cyclone,

    A man might parry ;
But only faith, or 'triple brass,'
Can help the 'outward-bound' to pass
Safe through that eastward-faring class

    Who sail to marry.

III.

For him fond mothers, stout and fair,
Ascend the tortuous cabin stair
Only to hold around his chair

    Insidious sessions;
For him the eyes of daughters droop
Across the plate of handed soup,
Suggesting seats upon the poop,

    And soft confessions.

IV.

Nor are these all his pains, nor most.

Romancing captains cease to boast—

Loud majors leave their whist—to roast

    The youthful griffin ;

All, all with pleased persistence show

His fate,—'remote, unfriended, slow,'—

His 'melancholy' bungalow,—

    His lonely tiffin.

V.

In vain.   Let doubts assail the weak ;

Unmoved and calm as 'Adam's Peak,'

Your 'blameless Arthur' hears them speak

    Of woes that wait him ;

Nought can subdue his soul secure ;

'Arthur will come again,' be sure,

Though matron shrewd and maid mature

    Conspire to mate him.

VI.

But, Laura, on your side, forbear

To greet with too impressed an air

A certain youth with chesnut hair,—

A youth unstable ;

Albeit none more skilled can guide

The frail canoe on Thamis tide,

Or, trimmer-footed, lighter glide

Through 'Guards'' or 'Mabel.'

VII.

Be warned in time.   Without a trace

Of acquiescence on your face,

Hear, in the waltz's breathing space,

His airy patter ;

Avoid the confidential nook ;

If, when you sing, you find his look

Grow tender, close your music-book,

And end the matter.

TO 'LYDIA LANGUISH.'

' *Il me faut des émotions.*'

BLANCHE AMORY.

I.

You ask me, Lydia, 'whether I,

If you refuse my suit, shall die.'

   (Now pray don't let this hurt you) ;

Although the time be out of joint,

I should not think a bodkin's point

   The sole resource of virtue ;

Nor shall I, though your mood endure,

Attempt a final Water-cure

   Except against my wishes ;

For I respectfully decline

To dignify the Serpentine,

    And make *hors-d'œuvres* for fishes :

But, if you ask me whether I

    Composedly can go,

Without a look, without a sigh,

    Why, then I answer—No.

II.

' You are assured,' you sadly say

(If in this most considerate way

    To treat my suit your will is),

That I shall ' quickly find as fair

Some new Neæra's tangled hair—

    Some easier Amaryllis.'

I cannot promise to be cold

If smiles are kind as yours of old

    On lips of later beauties ;

Nor can I hope to quite forget

The homage that is Nature's debt,

   While man has social duties ;

But, if you ask shall I prefer

   To you I honour so

A somewhat visionary Her,

   I answer truly—No.

III.

You fear, you frankly add, ' to find

In me too late the altered mind

   That altering Time estranges.'

To this I make response that we

(As physiologists agree),

   Must have septennial changes ;

This is a thing beyond control,

And it were best upon the whole

   To try and find out whether

We could not, by some means, arrange

This not-to-be-avoided change

   So as to change together :

But, had you asked me to allow

   That you could ever grow

Less amiable than you are now,—

   Emphatically—No.

IV.

But—to be serious—if you care

To know how I shall really bear

   This much-discussed rejection,

I answer you.   As feeling men

Behave, in best romances, when

   You outrage their affection ;—

With that gesticulatory woe,

By which, as melodramas show,

   Despair is indicated ;

Enforced by all the liquid grief

Which hugest pocket-handkerchief

   Has ever simulated ;

And when, arrived so far, you say

   In tragic accents ' Go,'

Then, Lydia, then—I still shall stay,

   And firmly answer No.

GROWING GRAY.

'*On a l'âge de son cœur.*'
A. D'HOUDETOT.

A LITTLE more toward the light ;—

Me miserable ! Here's one that's white ;

And one that's turning ;

Adieu to song and ' salad days ;'

My muse, let's go at once to Jay's,

And order mourning.

We must reform our rhymes, my Dear,—

Renounce the gay for the severe,—

Be grave, not witty ;

We have, no more, the right to find
That Pyrrha's hair is neatly twined,—
    That Chloe's pretty.

Young Love's for us a farce that's played ;
Light canzonet and serenade
    No more may tempt us ;
Gray hairs but ill accord with dreams ;
From aught but sour didactic themes
    Our years exempt us.

' *A la bonne heure !* ' You fancy so ?
You think for one white streak we grow
    At once satiric ?
A fiddlestick ! Each hair's a string
To which our greybeard Muse shall sing
    A younger lyric.

The heart's still sound.   Shall ' cakes and ale '

Grow rare to youth because *we* rail

   At schoolboy dishes ?

Perish the thought !   'Tis ours to sing

When neither Time nor Tide can bring

   Belief with wishes.

LOVE IN WINTER.

Between the berried holly-bush
The Blackbird whistled to the Thrush:
'Which way did bright-eyed Bella go?
Look, Speckle-breast, across the snow,—
Are those her dainty tracks I see,
That wind toward the shrubbery?'

The Throstle pecked the berries still.
'No need for looking, Yellow-bill;
Young Frank was there an hour ago,
Half-frozen, waiting in the snow;
His callow beard was white with rime,—
Tchuck,—'tis a merry pairing-time!'

'What would you?' twittered in the Wren;

'These are the reckless ways of men.

I watched them bill and coo as though

They thought the sign of Spring was snow;

If men but timed their loves as we,

'Twould save this inconsistency.'

'Nay, Gossip,' chirped the Robin, 'nay;

I like their unreflective way.

Besides, I heard enough to show

Their love is proof against the snow :—

Why wait, he said, *why wait for May,*

When love can warm a winter's day? '

POT-POURRI.

' Si jeunesse savait! —'

I PLUNGE my hand among the leaves :
(An alien touch but dust perceives,
　　Nought else supposes ;)
For me those fragrant ruins raise
Clear memory of the vanished days
　　When they were roses.

' If youth but knew !'　Ah, ' if,' in truth —
I can recall with what gay youth,
　　To what light chorus,
Unsobered yet by time or change,
We roamed the many-gabled Grange,
　　All life before us ;

Braved the old clock-tower's dust and damp
To catch the dim Arthurian camp
    In misty distance ;
Peered at the still-room's sacred stores,
Or rapped at walls for sliding doors
    Of feigned existence.

Vogue la galère ! What need for cares !
The hot sun parched the old parterres
    And 'flowerful closes ;'
We roused the rooks with rounds and glees,
Played hide-and-seek behind the trees,—
    Then plucked these roses.

Louise was one—light, glib Louise,
So freshly freed from school decrees
    You scarce could stop her ;
And Bell, the Beauty, unsurprised
At fallen locks that scandalized
    Our dear ' Miss Proper :'—

Shy Ruth, all heart and tenderness,
Who wept—like Chaucer's Prioress,
    When Dash was smitten ;
Who blushed before the mildest men,
Yet waxed a very Corday when
    You teased her kitten.

I loved them all.   Bell first and best ;
Louise the next—for days of jest,
    Or madcap masking ;
And Ruth, I thought,—why, failing these,
When my High-Mightiness should please,
    She 'd come for asking.

Louise was grave when last we met ;
Bell's beauty, like a sun, has set ;
    And Ruth, Heaven bless her,
Ruth that I wooed,—and wooed in vain,
Has gone where neither grief nor pain
    Can now distress her.

DOROTHY.

A REVERIE.

(Suggested by the name upon a Pane.)

SHE then must once have looked, as I
Look now, across the level rye,—
Past Church and Manor-house, and seen,
As now I see, the village green,
The bridge, and Walton's river—she
Whose old-world name was ' Dorothy.'

The swallows must have twittered, too,
Above her head ; the roses blew
Below, no doubt,—and, sure, the South
Crept up the wall and kissed her mouth,—

That wistful mouth, which comes to me
Linked with her name of Dorothy.

What was she like?   I picture her
Unmeet for uncouth worshipper ;—
Soft,—pensive,—far too subtly graced
To suit the blunt bucolic taste,
Whose crude perception could but see
' Ma'am Fine-airs' in ' Miss Dorothy.'

How not?   She loved, may be, perfume,
Soft textures, lace, a half-lit room ;—
Perchance too candidly preferred
' Clarissa ' to a gossip's word ;—
And, for the rest, would seem to be
Or proud or dull—this Dorothy.

Poor child—with heart the down-lined nest
Of warmest instincts unconfest,

Soft, callow things that vaguely felt

The breeze caress, the sunlight melt,

But yet, by some obscure decree

Unwinged from birth ;—poor Dorothy !

Not less I dream her mute desire

To acred churl and booby squire,

Now pale, with timorous eyes that filled

At ' twice-told tales' of foxes killed ;—

Now trembling when slow tongues grew free

'Twixt sport, and Port—and Dorothy !

'Twas then she 'd seek this nook, and find

Its evening landscape balmy-kind ;

And here, where still her gentle name

Lives on the old green glass, would frame

Fond dreams of unfound harmony

'Twixt heart and heart.   Poor Dorothy !

L'ENVOI.

These last I spoke.   Then Florence said,

Below me,—'Dreams? Delusions, Fred!'

Next, with a pause,—she bent the while

Over a rose, with roguish smile—

'But how disgusted, sir, you'll be

To hear *I* scrawled that "Dorothy."'

A CITY FLOWER.

' Il y a des fleurs animées.'

POLITE COLLOQUIALISM.

I.

To and fro in the City I go,

Tired of the ceaseless ebb and flow,

  Sick of the crowded mart ;

Tired of the din and rattle of wheels,

Sick of the dust as one who feels

  The dust is over his heart.

II.

And again and again, as the sunlight wanes,

I think of the lights in the leafy lanes,

   With the bits of blue between ;

And when about Rimmel's the perfumes play,

I smell no odour of ' Ess Bouquet,'

   But violets hid in the green ;

And I love—how I love !—the plants that fill

The pots on my dust-dry window-sill,—

   A sensitive sickly crop,—

But a flower that charms me more, I think,

Than cowslip, or crocus, or rose, or pink,

   Blooms—in a milliner's shop.

III.

Hazel eyes that wickedly peep,

Flash, abash, and suddenly sleep

   Under the lids drawn in ;

Ripple of hair that rioteth out,

Mouth with a half-born smile and a pout,

And a baby breadth of chin ;

Hands that light as the lighting bird,

On the bloom-bent bough, and the bough

stirred

With a delicate ecstasy ;

Fingers tipped with a roseate flush,

Flicking and flirting a feathery brush

Over the papery bonnetry ;—

Till the gauzy rose begins to glow,

And the gauzy hyacinths break and blow,

And the dusty grape grows red ;

And the flaunting grasses seem to say,

'Do we look like ornaments—tell us, we pray

Fit for a lady's head ?'

And the butterfly wakes to a wiry life,

Like an elderly gentleman taking a wife,

Knowing he must be gay ;

And all the bonnets nid-noddle about,

Like chattering chaperons set at a rout,

    Quarrelling over their play.

IV.

How can I otherwise choose than look

At the beautiful face like a beautiful book,

    And learn a tiny part?

So I feel somehow that every day

Some flake of the dust is brushed away

    That had settled over my heart.

K

INCOGNITA.

I.

Just for a space that I met her —
  Just for a day in the train !
It began when she feared it would wet her,
  That tiniest spurtle of rain :
So we tucked a great rug in the sashes,
  And carefully padded the pane ;
And I sorrow in sackcloth and ashes,
  Longing to do it again !

II.

Then it grew when she begged me to reach her

    A dressing-case under the seat ;

She was 'really so tiny a creature,

    That she needed a stool for her feet ! '

Which was promptly arranged to her order

    With a care that was even minute,

And a glimpse—of an open-work border,

    And a glance—of the fairyest boot.

III.

Then it drooped, and revived at some hovels—

    'Were they houses for men or for pigs ? '

Then it shifted to muscular novels,

    With a little digression on prigs :

She thought 'Wives and Daughters ' ' *so* jolly ;

    ' Had I read it ? ' She knew when I had,

Like the rest, I should dote upon ' Molly ; '

    And ' poor Mrs. Gaskell—how sad ! '

IV.

'Like Browning?' 'But so-so.'   His proof lay

   Too deep for her frivolous mood,

That preferred your mere metrical *soufflé*

   To the stronger poetical food;

Yet at times he was good—'as a tonic :'

   Was Tennyson writing just now?

And was this new poet Byronic,

   And clever, and naughty, or how?

V.

Then we trifled with concerts and croquêt,

   Then she daintily dusted her face;

Then she sprinkled herself with 'Ess Bouquet,'

   Fished out from the foregoing case;

And we chattered of Gassier and Grisi,

   And voted Aunt Sally a bore;

Discussed if the tight rope were easy,

   Or Chopin much harder than Spohr.

VI.

And oh ! the odd things that she quoted,

  With the prettiest possible look,

And the price of two buns that she noted

  In the prettiest possible book ;

While her talk like a musical rillet

  Flashed on with the hours that flew,

And the carriage, her smile seemed to fill it

  With just enough summer—for Two.

VII.

Till at last in her corner, peeping

  From a nest of rugs and of furs,

With the white shut eyelids sleeping

  On those dangerous looks of hers,

She seemed like a snowdrop breaking,

  Not wholly alive nor dead,

But with one blind impulse making

  To the sounds of the spring overhead ;

VIII.

And I watched in the lamplight's swerving
The shade of the down-dropt lid,
And the lip-line's delicate curving,
Where a slumbering smile lay hid,
Till I longed that, rather than sever,
The train should shriek into space,
And carry us onward—for ever,—
Me and that beautiful face.

IX.

But she suddenly woke in a fidget,
With fears she was ' nearly at home,'
And talk of a certain Aunt Bridget,
Whom I mentally wished—well at Rome ;
Got out at the very next station,
Looking back with a merry *Bon Soir*,
Adding, too, to my utter vexation,
A surplus, unkind *Au Revoir*.

X.

So left me to muse on her graces,

    To doze and to muse, till I dreamed

That we sailed through the sunniest places

    In a glorified galley, it seemed ;

But the cabin was made of a carriage,

    And the ocean was Eau-de-Cologne,

And we split on a rock labelled MARRIAGE,

    And I woke,—as cold as a stone.

XI.

And that's how I lost her—a jewel—

    Incognita—one in a crowd,

Not prudent enough to be cruel,

    Not worldly enough to be proud.

It was just a shut lid and its lashes,

    Just a few hours in a train,

And I sorrow in sackcloth and ashes

    Longing to see her again !

MY LANDLADY.

A SMALL brisk woman, capped with many a bow;
    'Yes,' so she says, 'and younger, too, than some,'
Who bids me, bustling, 'God speed,' when I go,
    And gives me, rustling, 'Welcome' when I come.

' Ay, sir, 'tis cold,—and freezing hard,—they say;
    I 'd like to give that hulking brute a hit
Beating his horse in such a shameful way !—
    Step here, sir, till your fire 's blazed up a bit.'

A musky haunt of lavender and shells,
    Quaint-figured Chinese monsters, toys, and trays—
A life's collection—where each object tells
    Of fashions gone and half-forgotten ways :—

A glossy screen, where wide-mouth dragons ramp ;

    A vexed inscription in a sampler-frame ;

A shade of beads upon a red-capped lamp ;

    A child's mug graven with a golden name ;

A pictured ship, with full-blown canvas set ;

    A cord, with sea-weed twisted to a wreath,

Circling a silky curl as black as jet,

    With yellow writing faded underneath.

Looking, I sink within the shrouded chair,

    And note the objects slowly, one by one,

And light at last upon a portrait there,—

    Wide-collared, raven-haired. ' Yes, 'tis my son ! '

' Where is he ?' ' Ah, Sir, he is dead—my boy !

    Nigh ten long years ago—in 'sixty-three ;

He 's always living in my head—my boy !

    He was left drowning in the Southern Sea.

' There were two souls washed overboard, they said,
  And one the waves brought back ; but he was left
They saw him place the life-buoy o'er his head ;
  The sea was running wildly ;—he was left.

' He was a strong, strong swimmer.   Do you know,
  When the wind whistled yesternight, I cried,
And prayed to God, though 'twas so long ago,
  He did not struggle much before he died.

' 'Twas his third voyage. That's the box he brought,—
  Or would have brought—my poor deserted boy !
And these the words the agents sent—they thought
  That money, perhaps, could make my loss a joy.

' Look, Sir, I 've something here that I prize more :
  This is a fragment of the poor lad's coat,—
That other clutched him as the wave went o'er,
  And this stayed in his hand. That 's what they wrote.

' Well, well, 'tis done.   My story's shocking you ;—

Grief is for them that have both time and wealth :

We can't mourn much, who have much work to do ;

Your fire is bright.   Thank God, I have my health !

THE DRAMA OF THE DOCTOR'S WINDOW.

IN THREE ACTS, WITH A PROLOGUE.

A tedious brief scene of young Pyramus,
And his love Thisbe; very tragical mirth.
MIDSUMMER-NIGHT'S DR

PROLOGUE.

I.

' WELL, I must wait!' The Doctor's room,

Where I used this expression,

Wore the severe official gloom

Attached to that profession;

Rendered severer by a bald

And skinless Gladiator,

Whose raw robustness first appalled

The entering spectator.

II.

No one would call 'The Lancet' gay,—
   Few could avoid confessing
That Jones, 'On Muscular Decay,'
   Is, as a rule, depressing :
So, leaving both, to change the scene,
   I turned toward the shutter,
And peered out vacantly between
   A water-butt and gutter.

III.

Below, the Doctor's garden lay,
   If thus imagination
May dignify a square of clay
   Unused to vegetation,
Filled with a dismal-looking swing—
   That brought to mind a gallows—
An empty kennel, mouldering,
   And two dyspeptic aloes.

IV.

No sparrow chirped, no daisy sprung,

. About the place deserted ;

Only across the swing-board hung

A battered doll, inverted,

Which sadly seemed to disconcert

The vagrant cat that scanned it,

Sniffed doubtfully around the skirt,

But failed to understand it.

V.

A dreary spot !   And yet, I own,

Half-hoping that, perchance, it

Might, in some unknown way, atone

For Jones and for ' The Lancet,'

I watched ; and by especial grace,

Within this stage contracted,

Saw presently before my face

A classic story acted.

VI.

Ah, World of ours, are you so gray

 And weary, World, of spinning,

That you repeat the tales to-day

 You told at the beginning ?

For lo ! the same old myths that made

 The early ' stage successes,'

Still ' hold the boards,' and still are played,

 ' With new effects and dresses.'

VII.

Small, lonely ' three-pair-backs' behold,

 To-day, Alcestis dying ;

To-day, in farthest Polar cold,

 Ulysses' bones are lying ;

Still in one's morning ' Times ' one reads

 How fell an Indian Hector ;

Still clubs discuss Achilles' steeds,

 Briseis' next protector ;—

VIII.

Still Menelaus brings, we see,

His oft-remanded case on ;

Still somewhere sad Hypsipyle

Bewails a faithless Jason ;

And here, the Doctor's sill beside,

Do I not now discover

A Thisbe, whom the walls divide

From Pyramus, her lover ?

ACT THE FIRST.

IX.

Act I. began.   Some noise had scared

The cat, that like an arrow

Shot up the wall and disappeared ;

And then across the narrow,

Unweeded path, a small dark thing,

Hid by a garden-bonnet,

Passed wearily towards the swing,

Paused, turned, and climbed upon it.

X.

A child of five, with eyes that were

    At least a decade older,

A mournful mouth, and tangled hair

    Flung careless round her shoulder,

Dressed in a stiff ill-fitting frock,

    Whose black uncomely rigour

Seemed to sardonically mock

    The plaintive, slender figure.

XI.

What was it? Something in the dress

    That told the girl unmothered;

Or was it that the merciless

    Black garb of mourning smothered

Life and all light :—but rocking so,

    In the dull garden-corner,

The lonely swinger seemed to grow

    More piteous and forlorner.

L

XII.

Then, as I looked, across the wall

Of ' next-door's ' garden, that is—

To speak correctly—through its tall

Surmounting fence of lattice,

Peeped a boy's face, with curling hair,

Ripe lips, half-drawn asunder,

And round, bright eyes, that wore a stare

Of frankest childish wonder.

XIII.

Rounder they grew by slow degrees,

Until the swinger, swerving,

Made, all at once, alive to these

Intentest orbs observing,

Gave just one brief, half-uttered cry,

And,—as with gathered kirtle,

Nymphs fly from Pan's head suddenly

Thrust through the budding myrtle,—

XIV.

Fled in dismay.   A moment's space,

   The eyes looked almost tragic ;

Then, when they caught my watching face,

   Vanished as if by magic ;

And, like some sombre thing beguiled

   To strange, unwonted laughter,

The gloomy garden having smiled,

   Became the gloomier after.

ACT THE SECOND.

XV.

Yes : they were gone, the stage was bare,—

   Blank as before ; and therefore,

Sinking within the patient's chair,

   Half vexed, I knew not wherefore,

I dozed ; till, startled by some call,

   A glance sufficed to show me,

The boy again above the wall,

   The girl erect below me.

XVI.

The boy, it seemed, to add a force
　　To words found unavailing,
Had pushed a striped and spotted horse
　　Half through the blistered paling,
Where now it stuck, stiff-legged and straigh
　　While he, in exultation,
Chattered some half-articulate
　　Excited explanation.

XVII.

Meanwhile, the girl, with upturned face,
　　Stood motionless, and listened ;
The ill-cut frock had gained a grace,
　　The pale hair almost glistened ;
The figure looked alert and bright,
　　Buoyant as though some power
Had lifted it, as rain at night
　　Uplifts a drooping flower.

XVIII.

The eyes had lost their listless way,—
　　The old life, tired and faded,
Had slipped down with the doll that lay
　　Before her feet, degraded ;
She only, yearning upward, found
　　In those bright eyes above her
The ghost of some enchanted ground
　　Where even Nurse would love her.

XIX.

Ah, tyrant Time ! you hold the book,
　　We, sick and sad, begin it ;
You close it fast, if we but look
　　Pleased for a meagre minute ;
You closed it now, for, out of sight,
　　Some warning finger beckoned ;
Exeunt both to left and right ;—
　　Thus ended Act the Second.

ACT THE THIRD.

XX.

Or so it proved.   For while I still

　Believed them gone for ever,

Half-raised above the window sill,

　I saw the lattice quiver;

And lo, once more appeared the head,

　Flushed, while the round mouth pouted

'Give Tom a kiss,' the red lips said, .

　In style the most undoubted.

XXI.

The girl came back without a thought;

　Dear Muse of Mayfair, pardon,

If more restraint had not been taught

　In this neglected garden;

For these your code was all too stiff,

　So, seeing none dissented,

Their unfeigned faces met as if

　Manners were not invented.

XXII.

Then on the scene,—by happy fate,

When lip from lip had parted,

And, therefore, just two seconds late,—

A sharp-faced nurse-maid darted ;

Swooped on the boy, as swoops a kite

Upon a rover chicken,

And bore him sourly off, despite

His well-directed kicking.

XXIII.

The girl stood silent, with a look

Too subtle to unravel,

Then, with a sudden gesture took

The torn doll from the gravel ;

Hid the whole face, with one caress,

Under the garden bonnet,

And, passing in, I saw her press

Kiss after kiss upon it.

Exeunt omnes.   End of play.

It made the dull room brighter,

The Gladiator almost gay,

And e'en 'The Lancet' lighter.

AN UNFINISHED SONG.

' Cantat Deo qui vivit Deo.'

YES, he was well-nigh gone and near his rest,
  The year could not renew him ; nor the cry
Of building nightingales about the nest ;
  Nor that soft freshness of the May-wind's sigh,

That fell before the garden scents, and died
  Between the ampler leafage of the trees :
All these he knew not, lying open-eyed,
  Deep in a dream that was not pain nor ease,

But death not yet.   Outside a woman talked—
  His wife she was—whose clicking needles sped
To faded phrases of complaint that balked
  My rising words of comfort.   Overhead,

A cage that hung amid the jasmine stars
  Trembled a little, and a blossom dropped.
Then notes came pouring through the wicker bars,
  Climbed half a rapid arc of song, and stopped.

' Is it a thrush ?' I asked.   ' A thrush,' she said.
  ' That was Will's tune.   Will taught him that befo
He left the doorway settle for his bed,
  Sick as you see, and couldn't teach him more.

' He 'd bring his Bible here o' nights, would Will,
  Following the light, and whiles when it was dark
And days were warm, he 'd sit there' whistling still,
  Teaching the bird.   He whistled like a lark.'

'Jack! Jack!' A joyous flutter stirred the cage,

   Shaking the blossoms down. The bird began ;

The woman turned again to want and wage,

   And in the inner chamber sighed the man.

How clear the song was! Musing as I heard,

   My fancies wandered from the droning wife

To sad comparison of man and bird,—

   The broken song, the uncompleted life,

That seemed a broken song; and of the two,

   My thought a moment deemed the bird more blest,

That, when the sun shone, sang the notes it knew,

   Without desire or knowledge of the rest.

Nay, happier man. For him futurity

   Still hides a hope that this his earthly praise

Finds heavenly end, for surely will not He,

   Solver of all, above his Flower of Days,

Teach him the song that no one living knows?

    Let the man die, with that half-chant of his,—

What Now discovers not Hereafter shows,

    And God will surely teach him more than this.

Again the bird.   I turned, and passed along;

    But Time and Death, Eternity and Change,

Talked with me ever, and the climbing song

    Rose in my hearing, beautiful and strange.

THE SUNDIAL.

'Tis an old dial, dark with many a stain ;
   In summer crowned with drifting orchard bloom,
Tricked in the autumn with the yellow rain,
   And white in winter like a marble tomb ;

And round about its gray, time-eaten brow
   Lean letters speak—a worn and shattered row :
I am a Shade: a Shadowe too arte thou :
   I marke the Time: saye, Gossip, dost thou soe ?

Here would the ringdoves linger, head to head ;

And here the snail a silver course would run,

Beating old Time ; and here the peacock spread

His gold-green glory, shutting out the sun.

The tardy shade moved forward to the noon ;

Betwixt the paths a dainty Beauty stept,

That swung a flower, and, smiling, hummed a
tune,—

Before whose feet a barking spaniel leapt.

O'er her blue dress an endless blossom strayed ;

About her tendril-curls the sunlight shone ;

And round her train the tiger-lilies swayed,

Like courtiers bowing till the queen be gone.

She leaned upon the slab a little while,

Then drew a jewelled pencil from her zone,

Scribbled a something with a frolic smile,

Folded, inscribed, and niched it in the stone.

The shade slipped on, no swifter than the snail ;
　There came a second lady to the place,
Dove-eyed, dove-robed, and something wan and
　　pale—
　An inner beauty shining from her face.

She, as if listless with a lonely love,
　Straying among the alleys with a book,—
Herrick or Herbert,—watched the circling dove,
　And spied the tiny letter in the nook.

Then, like to one who confirmation found
　Of some dread secret half-accounted true,—
Who knew what hands and hearts the letter bound,
　And argued loving commerce 'twixt the two,

She bent her fair young forehead on the stone ;
　The dark shade gloomed an instant on her head ;
And 'twixt her taper-fingers pearled and shone
　The single tear that tear-worn eyes will shed.

The shade slipped onward to the falling gloom ;

    There came a soldier gallant in her stead,

Swinging a beaver with a swaling plume,

    A ribboned love-lock rippling from his head ;

Blue-eyed, frank-faced, with clear and open brow

    Scar-seamed a little, as the women love ;

So kindly fronted that you marvelled how

    The frequent sword-hilt had so frayed his glov

Who switched at Psyche plunging in the sun ;

    Uncrowned three lilies with a backward swing

And standing somewhat widely, like to one

    More used to ' Boot and Saddle ' than to cring

As courtiers do, but gentleman withal,

    Took out the note ;—held it as one who feare(

The fragile thing he held would slip and fall ;

    Read and re-read, pulling his tawny beard ;

Kissed it, I think, and hid it in his breast ;

Laughed softly in a flattered happy way,

Arranged the broidered baldrick on his chest,

And sauntered past, singing a roundelay.

.   .   .   .   .

The shade crept forward through the dying glow ;

There came no more nor dame nor cavalier ;

But for a little time the brass will show

A small gray spot—the record of a tear.

M

THE SICK MAN AND THE BIRDS.

ÆGROTUS.

SPRING,—art thou come, O Spring!

   I am too sick for words;

How hast thou heart to sing,

   O Spring, with all thy birds?

MERULA.

I sing for joy to see again

The merry leaves along the lane,

   The little bud grown ripe;

And look, my love upon the bough!

Hark, how she calleth to me now,—

          ' Pipe! pipe!'

ÆGROTUS.

Ah ! weary is the sun :

    Love is an idle thing ;

But, Bird, thou restless one,

    What ails thee, wandering ?

HIRUNDO.

By shore and sea I come and go

To seek I know not what ; and lo !

    On no man's eaves I sit

But voices bid me rise once more,

To flit again by sea and shore,—

        Flit ! Flit !

ÆGROTUS.

This is Earth's bitter cup :—

    Only to seek, not know.

But Thou, that strivest up,

    Why dost thou carol so ?

ALAUDA.

A secret Spirit gifteth me

With song, and wing that lifteth me,—

A Spirit for whose sake,

Striving amain to reach the sky,

Still to the old dark earth I cry—

'Wake! wake!'

ÆGROTUS.

My hope hath lost its wing.

Thou, that to Night dost call,

How hast thou heart to sing

Thy tears made musical?

PHILOMELA.

Alas for me! a dry desire

Is all my song,—a waste of fire

That will not fade nor fail;

To me, dim shapes of ancient crime

Moan through the windy ways of time,

'Wail! wail!'

ÆGROTUS.

Thine is the sick man's song,—

Mournful, in sooth, and fit;

Unrest that cries 'How long!'—

And the Night answers it.

THE DEATH OF PROCRIS.

A VERSION SUGGESTED BY THE SO-NAMED PICTURE C
PIERO DI COSIMO, IN THE NATIONAL GALLERY.

PROCRIS, the nymph, had wedded Cephalus ;—

He, till the spring had warmed to slow-winged day

Heavy with June, untired and amorous,

Named her his love ; but now, in unknown ways

His heart was gone ; and evermore his gaze

Turned from her own, and ever farther ranged

His woodland war ; while she, in dull amaze,

Beholding with the hours her husband changed,

Sighed for his lost caress, by some hard god estrange

So, on a day, she rose and found him not.

Alone, with wet, sad eye, she watched the shade.

Brighten below a soft-rayed sun that shot

Arrows of light through all the deep-leaved glade ;

Then, with weak hands, she knotted up the braid

Of her brown hair, and o'er her shoulders cast

Her crimson weed ; with faltering fingers made

Her golden girdle's clasp to join, and past

Down to the trackless wood, full pale and overcast.

And all day long her slight spear devious flew,

And harmless swerved her arrows from their aim,

For ever, as the ivory bow she drew,

Before her ran the still unwounded game.

Then, at the last, a hunter's cry there came,

And, lo, a hart that panted with the chase,

Thereat her cheek was lightened as with flame,

And swift she gat her to a leafy place,

Thinking, ' I yet may chance unseen to see his face.'

Leaping he went, this hunter Cephalus,

Bent in his hand his cornel bow he bare,

Supple he was, round-limbed and vigorous,

Fleet as his dogs, a lean Laconian pair.

He, when he spied the brown of Procris' hair

Move in the covert, deeming that apart

Some fawn lay hidden, loosed an arrow there;

Nor cared to turn and seek the speeded dart,

Bounding above the fern, fast following up the ha

But Procris lay among the white wind-flowers,

Shot in the throat.   From out the little wound

The slow blood drained, as drops in autumn shot

Drip from the leaves upon the sōdden ground.

None saw her die but Lelaps, the swift hound,

That watched her dumbly with a wistful fear,

Till, at the dawn, the hornèd wood-men found

And bore her gently on a sylvan bier,

To lie beside the sea, with many an uncouth tear.

PALOMYDES.

I.

Him best in all the dim Arthuriad,
  Of lovers of fair women, him I prize,—
The Pagan Palomydes.   Never glad
  Was he with sweetness of his lady's eyes,
    Nor joy he had.

II.

But, unloved ever, still must love the same,
  And riding ever through a lonely world,
Whene'er on adverse shield or crest he came,
  Against the danger desperately hurled,
    Crying her name.

III.

So I, who strove to You I may not earn,

Methinks, am come unto so high a place,

That though from hence I can but vainly yearn

For that averted favour of your face,

I shall not turn.

IV.

No, I am come too high. Whate'er betide,

To find the doubtful thing that fights with n

Toward the mountain tops I still shall ride,

And cry your name in my extremity,

As Palomyde,

V.

Until the issue come. Will it disclose

No gift of grace, no pity made complete,

After much labour done,—much war with wo(

Will you deny me still in Heaven, my sweet

Ah, Death—who knows ?

A SONG OF ANGIOLA ON EARTH.

THIS is my Lady's throne :—

 Among green leaves, in bowers

  From sunlight fenced with care

By great boughs overgrown ;

 Her feet are deep in flowers,

  They fall around her hair ;

There is no bird nor sylvan thing

But stays to listen, if she sing

  Before I seek her there.

This is my Lady's face :—

 A cloud of yellow hair

  Stands round about her ear ;

She hath a mouth of grace,

A forehead white and fair,

And blue eyes very clear ;

Lids that go over while I see,

And shut the world away from me,

Because she is so dear.

This is my Lady's dress :—

In fine silk fairly fit,

Blue as an egg is she ;

Broad bands her shoulders press

With dark devices knit,

And small pearls curiously.

A silver girdle holds her waist,

Whereon these words are rightly traced :—

A true man taketh me.

This is my Lady's name :—

It is as soft as air,

As sweet as is the rose ;

No other sounds the same,

 No song is half so fair,

  No music's dying close ;—

But yet, methinks, 'twere sin to say

My Lady's name in open day

  For him to speak who knows.

This is my Lady's praise :—

 Shame before her is shamed,

  Hate cannot hate repeat ;

She is so pure of ways

 There is no sin is named

  But falls before her feet ;

Because she is so frankly free,

So tender and so good to see,

  Because she is so sweet.

This is my love of her :—

 It waxeth ever new,

  Nor waneth any whit ;

This all my heart doth stir,
     Just that I may be true
          And as she findeth fit;
There is no thing she bids me do
But I would die to bear it through
     Because she asketh it.

Sweet-swelling song of mine,
     Take cassia, balm, and nard;
          Then hie thee fast with care,
Find out my Lady sweet,
With delicate white feet:
Before her feet incline,
     And kiss them—kiss them hard,
          And wipe them with thine hair,
Saying 'My Master bids thee know,
Madonna, that he greets thee so,
     Seeing thou art so fair.'

A FLOWER SONG OF ANGIOLA.

Down where the garden grows,
  Gay as a banner,
Spake to her mate the Rose
  After this manner :—
' We are the first of flowers,
  Plain-land or hilly,
All reds and whites are ours,
  Are they not, Lily ?'

Then to the flowers I spake,—
  'Watch ye my Lady
Gone to the leafy brake,
  Silent and shady ;

When I am near to her,

    Lily, she knows;

How I am dear to her,

    Look to it, Rose.'

•

Straightway the Blue-bell stooped,

    Paler for pride,

Down where the Violet drooped,

    Shy, at her side :—

' Sweetheart, save me and you,

    Where has the summer kist

Flowers of as fair a hue,—

    Turkis or Amethyst ? '

Therewith I laughed aloud,

    Spake on this wise,

' O little flowers so proud,

    Have ye seen eyes

Change through the blue in them,—

Change till the mere

Loving that grew in them

Turned to a tear ? '

' Flowers, ye are bright of hue,

Delicate, sweet ;

Flowers, and the sight of you

Lightens men's feet ;

Yea ; but her worth to me,

Flowerets, even,

Sweetening the earth to me,

Sweeteneth heaven.

This, then, O Flowers, I sing ;

God, when He made ye

Made yet a fairer thing

Making my Lady ;—

N

Fashioned her tenderly,

　　Giving all weal to her ;—

Girdle ye slenderly,

　　Go to her, kneel to her,—

Saying, " He sendeth us,

　　He the most dutiful,

Meetly he endeth us,

　　Maiden most beautiful !

Let us get rest of you,

　　Sweet, in your breast ;—

Die, being prest of you,

　　Die, being blest." '

A SONG OF ANGIOLA DEAD.

SONG, art thou sad, my Song?

Thou hast not ease nor sleep,

Thou art not gay nor glad;

Hast thou not mourned too long?

Speak to me, song, nor weep

Till thou grow gray and mad

For that all Love is fled,

Beauty and bountihed ;—

Song, thou art sad.

Song, ah how fair was she !—

   Days but her praise repeat ;—

      Men may seek out with care

Nowhere such eyes to see,

   Nowhere such little feet,—

      Yea, and such yellow hair ;

Nowhere like lips, I weet

Kisses thereon to eat ;—

      Song, she was fair !

Song, and how sweet she was !

   Spring breezes kissed her face,

      Little leaves kissed her feet,

And the sun kissed, because

   Nowhere in any place

      Thing was to kiss so sweet ;

Nothing so dear as she,

Gentle and maidenly ;—

      Song, she was sweet !

Song, but how good she was !

There was no word she said,

But it was wise and good ;

No abject thing but has

Out from her mercy fed,

Strong in her pity stood ;

There was no little child

But to her leapt and smiled ;—

Song, she was good !

How shall we wait, my song ?

There is no mirth in cup,

Nowhere a feast is spread ;

Life is all marred and wrong,

Grief hath consumed it up,

Now that our Love is fled

Earth hath no face to see

Pointing my sword for me ;—

Song, she is dead !

Shall not we leave to sing ?

Nothing can wake her now,

Nothing can lift her head ;

There is no tune can bring

Back to her cheek and brow

Roses of white and red ;

Nothing of ours can stir

Words on the lips of her ;—

Song, she is dead !

'Cease then from scent, my song,

Change thee thy myrrh for rue,

Myrtle for calamus ;

Bring for us garments long,

Weeds to our grief, and strew

Dust on the hair of us,

For that all Love is fled

Beauty and bountihed ;—

Song, she is dead !

A SONG OF ANGIOLA IN HEAVEN.

FLOWERS,—that have died upon my Sweet

Lulled by the rhythmic dancing beat

    Of her young bosom under you,—

Now will I show you such a thing

As never, through thick buds of Spring,

    Betwixt the daylight and the dew,

The Bird whose being no man knows—

    The voice that waketh all night through,

        Tells to the Rose.

For lo,—a garden-place I found,

Well filled of leaves, and stilled of sound,

  Well flowered, with red fruit marvellous ;

And 'twixt the shining trunks would flit

Tall knights and silken maids, or sit

  With faces bent and amorous ;—

There, in the heart thereof, and crowned

  With woodbine and amaracus,

      My Love I found.

Alone she walked,—ah, well I wis,

My heart leapt up for joy of this !—

  Then when I called to her her name,—

The name, that like a pleasant thing

Men's lips remember, murmuring,

  At once across the sward she came,—

Full fain she seemed, my own dear maid,

  And askèd ever as she came,

      'Where hast thou stayed ?'

'Where hast thou stayed ?'—she asked as though

The long years were an hour ago ;

But I spake not, nor answerèd,

For, looking in her eyes, I saw,

A light not lit of mortal law ;

And in her clear cheeks' changeless red,

And sweet, unshaken speaking found

That in this place the Hours were dead,

And Time was bound.

'This is well done,'—she said,—'in thee,

O Love, that thou art come to me,

To this green garden glorious ;

Now truly shall our life be sped

In joyance and all goodlihed,

For here all things are fair to us,

And none with burden is oppressed,

And none is poor or piteous,—

For here is Rest.

'No formless Future blurs the sky ;

Men mourn not here, with dull dead eye,

  By shrouded shapes of Yesterday ;

Betwixt the Coming and the Past

The flawless life hangs fixen fast

  In one unwearying To-Day,

That darkens not ; for Sin is shriven,

    Death from the doors is thrust away,

        And here is Heaven.'

At 'Heaven' she ceased ;—and lifted up

Her fair head like a flower-cup,

  With rounded mouth, and eyes aglow ;

· Then set I lips to hers, and felt,—

Ah, God,—the hard pain fade and melt,

  And past things change to painted show ;

The song of quiring birds outbroke ;

    The lit leaves laughed,—sky shook, and lo,

        I swooned,—and woke.

And now, O Flowers,

    —Ye that indeed are dead,—

Now for all waiting hours,

    Well am I comforted;

For of a surety, now, I see,

      That, without dim distress

      Of tears, or weariness,

My Lady, verily, awaiteth me;

So that until with Her I be,

      For my dear Lady's sake

      I am right fain to make

Out from my pain a pillow, and to take

    Grief for a golden garment unto me;

      Knowing that I, at last, shall stand

      In that green garden-land,

And, in the holding of my dear Love's hand,

    Forget the grieving and the misery.

THE DYING OF TANNEGUY DU BOIS.

YEA, I am passed away, I think, from this ;

   Nor helps me herb, nor any leechcraft here,

But lift me hither the sweet cross to kiss,

   And witness ye, I go without a fear.

Yea, I am sped, and never more shall see,

   As once I dreamed, the show of shield and cre

Gone southward to the fighting by the sea ;—

   There is no bird in any last year's nest !

Yea, with me now all dreams are done, I ween,

    Grown faint and unremembered ; voices call

High up, like misty warders dimly seen

    Moving at morn on some Burgundian wall ;

And all things swim—as when the charger stands

    Quivering between the knees, and East and
        West

Are filled with flash of scarves and waving hands ;—

    There is no bird in any last year's nest !

Is she a dream I left in Acquitaine ?—

    My wife Giselle,—who never spoke a word,

Although I knew her mouth was drawn with pain,

    Her eyelids hung with tears ; and though I heard

The strong sob shake her throat, and saw the
        cord

    Her necklace made about it ;—she that prest

To watch me trotting till I reached the ford ;—

    There is no bird in any last year's nest.

Ah ! I had hoped, God wot,—had longed that s

  Should watch me from the little-lit tourelle,

Me, coming riding by the windy lea—

  Me, coming back again to her, Giselle ;

Yea, I had hoped once more to hear him call,

  The curly-pate, who, rushen lance in rest,

Stormed at the lilies by the orchard wall ;—

  There is no bird in any last year's nest !

But how, my Masters, ye are wrapt in gloom !

  This Death will come, and whom he loves he

    cleaves

Sheer through the steel and leather ; hating

  whom

  He smites in shameful wise behind the greave

'Tis a fair time with Dennis and the Saints,

  And weary work to age, and want for rest,

When harness groweth heavy, and one faints,

  With no bird left in any last year's nest !

Give ye good hap, then, all. For me, I lie

    Broken in Christ's sweet hand, with whom shall

        rest

To keep me living, now that I must die ;—

    There is no bird in any last year's nest !

THE BOOKWORM.

WE flung the close-kept casement wide ;
   The myriad atom-play
Streamed, with the mid-day's glancing tide,
   Across him as he lay ;
Only the unused summer gust
Moved the thin hair of Dryasdust.

The notes he writ were barely dry ;
   The entering breeze's breath
Fluttered the fruitless casuistry,
   Checked at the leaf where Death—
The final commentator—thrust
His cold 'Here endeth Dryasdust.'

O fool and blind ! The leaf that grew,
  The opening bud, the trees,
The face of men, he nowise knew,
  Or careless turned from these
To delve, in folios' rust and must,
The tomb he lived in, dry as dust.

He left, for mute Salmasius,
  The lore a child may teach,—
For saws of dead Libanius,
  The sound of uttered speech ;
No voice had pierced the sheep-skin crust
That bound the heart of Dryasdust.

And so, with none to close his eyes,
  And none to mourn him dead,
He in his dumb book-Babel lies
  With gray dust garmented.
Let be ; pass on. It is but just—
These were thy gods, O Dryasdust !

Dig we his grave where no birds greet,—

He loved no song of birds ;

Lay we his bones where no men meet,—

He loved no spoken words ;

He let his human-nature rust—

Write his *Hic Jacet* in the Dust.

THE PEACOCK ON THE WALL.

A MEDIÆVAL BALLAD, IN THE MODERN MANNER.

A DOUGHTY knight was Hue le Beau,
    A flower of men, perfay,
A gentle squire of dames also
    In his peculiar way.

I say ' peculiar,' for in truth,
    According to his view,
Men must have had eternal youth—
    Or nothing else to do.

He held that but when years had past
  In courtesies minute,
His love should yield herself at last
  To his protracted suit.

Culture, he urged, could love extend
  To lengths so undefined
A man might quite a lifetime spend
  Before he spoke his mind.

Alix le Fay was straight and tall,
  A maid of high degree ;
And by her father's orchard wall
  He met her,—frequently.

These were the merely prologue days,
  And on her lily cheek,
Sir Hue, for quite three hours, would gaze,
  But not a word would speak ;

Then, feeling first to ascertain
  Whether the grass was wet,
This blameless knight and man was fain
  Upon his knees to get ;

And lifting up her fingers two,
  With gentle gesture, he
Would lay his bearded lip thereto
  And kiss,—respectfully.

Seven years Sir Hue had gazed and kissed,
  In this enlightened wise,
And only on Saints' days had missed
  His usual exercise ;—

Seven years Sir Hue had kissed and gazed,
  And in no detail swerved,
Till he, one afternoon,—amazed,
  Perceived he was observed.

For lo, upon the orchard wall,

A Peacock-bird would rest,

That seemed to watch his motions all

With wonder manifest.

' Sir Knight,'—(at once began the bird),

' Though I appear abrupt,

Believe me that it ne'er occurred

To me to interrupt.

' Fair is the path of virtue traced

By men of low estate,

Much more, ennobled by the taste

And fancy of the great.

' A courtship, so refined, sedate

And singular in kind,

Could hardly fail to captivate

The well-conducted mind.

' Good hap, the highest and the least
      Can admiration stir,
And make of either bird or beast,
      A Hero-worshipper ;

' So I,—a bird—can yet revere
      The Beautiful—the True ;—
Permit me then, I pray, Messire,
      To join your party too,

' For you, I feel, will understand
      To closely contemplate
A suit so delicately planned,
      Must surely elevate.'

The Knight could not refuse request
      So gracefully preferred :
Thence, as the long amour progressed
      The blandly curious bird

Watched from the wall the varied shades
  Of ' Sweetness' and of ' Light,'
As good Sir Hue went through the grades
  Of Passion grown polite.

But, long ere Alix made him hers
  Departing from its post,
The Peacock, being full of years,
  Had yielded up the ghost ;

And after, when Sir Hue the maid
  By slow degrees had gained,
He had the circumstance portrayed
  Upon a window stained,

Showing himself, Alix le Fay,
  The Peacock watching by ;
' And there it stands unto this day
  To witness if I lie.'

NOTES.

NOTE I, PAGE 34.

An Incident in the Life of François Boucher.

See *Boucher* by Arsène Houssaye, *Galerie du* XVIIIE
Siècle (*Cinquième Série; Sculpteurs, Peintres, Musi-
ciens*).   The 'incident' is, however, thus briefly referred
to in Charles Blanc's *Histoire des Peintres de tous les
Écoles :*—' *Une fois cependant Boucher se laissa prendre
à un amour simple et candide.   Un jour, en passant dans
la Rue Ste.-Anne, il aperçut une jeune fruitière dont la
beauté l'éblouit.   C'était au temps des cerises.   Le peintre
la regarda et elle se laissa regarder sans songer à ses
paniers.   Ses lèvres parurent plus belles que ses cerises.
Un amour naïf et tendre naquit de cette échange de
regards; Boucher y trouva quelques jours de délices;
Rosine y trouva la mort après une rapide bonheur.*'

P

NOTE 2, PAGE 34.

The scene, a wood.

The picture referred to is *Le Panier Mystérieux* by F. Boucher ; engraved by R. Gaillard.

NOTE 3, PAGE 36.

And far afield were sun-baked savage creatures.

See *Les Caractères de* LA BRUYÈRE, *De l'homme.*

NOTE 4, PAGE 36.

Whose greatest grace was jupes à la Camargo.

'*C'était le beau temps où Camargo trouvait ses jupes trop longues pour danser la gargouillade.*'—ARSÈNE HOUSSAYE.

NOTE 5, PAGE 37.

The grass he called ' too green.'

'*Il trouvait la nature trop verte et mal éclairée. Et son ami Lancret, le peintre des salons à la mode, lui répondait : " Je suis de votre sentiment, la nature manque d'harmonie et de séduction."* '—CHARLES BLANC.

NOTE 6, PAGE 38.

Fresh as a fresh young pear-tree blossoming.

' She was wel more blisful on to see
Than is the newe perjenete tree.'

CHAUCER, *The Millere's Tale.*

NOTE 7, PAGE 47.

A Revolutionary Relic.

'373. ST. PIERRE (Bernardin de), *Paul et Virginie*, 12mo, old calf. Paris, 1787. This copy is pierced throughout by a bullet-hole, and bears on one of the covers the words :—"*à Lucile St. A. . . . . chez M. Batemans, à Edmonds-Bury, en Angleterre*," very faintly written in pencil.'—(Extract from Catalogue.)

NOTE 8, PAGE 51.

Did she wander like that other?

Lucile Desmoulins. See Carlyle's *French Revolution*, Book VI. chap ii.

NOTE 9, PAGE 53.

And its tender rain shall lave it.

It is by no means uncommon for an editor to interrupt some of these Revolutionary letters by a ' Here there are traces of tears.'

NOTE 10, PAGE 173.

I am a Shade : a Shadowe too art thou :
I marke the Time : saye, Gossip, dost thou soe ?
A motto in this spirit occurs at Stirling.

NOTE 11, PAGE 187.

A Song of Angiola on Earth.

It is perhaps scarcely necessary to state that this and the three pieces that follow owe their form and existence to the beautiful renderings of the Early Italian Poets (1100-1200-1300), by Mr. D. G. Rossetti, published in 1861.

NOTE 12, PAGE 199.

Flowers,—that have died upon my Sweet.

See *A Flower-Song of Angiola*, p. 191.

THE END.

EDINBURGH : T. AND A. CONSTABLE,
PRINTERS TO THE QUEEN, AND TO THE UNIVERSITY.

December, 1873.

A CATALOGUE OF

ENTERTAINING BOOKS

𝔉or 𝔓resents, an𝔡 for 𝔜oung 𝔓eople.

SELECTED FROM HENRY S. KING & CO.'S

CLASSIFIED CATALOGUE.

FOUR HANDSOME GIFT-BOOKS.

LYRICS OF LOVE FROM SHAKESPEARE TO TENNYSON. Selected and arranged by W. DAVENPORT ADAMS. Fcap. 8vo. Price 3*s.* 6*d.*

> "He has the prettiest love-songs for maids."—SHAKESPEARE.

Dedicated by Permission to the Poet Laureate.

WILLIAM CULLEN BRYANT'S POEMS. Handsomely bound. With Portrait of the Author. Price 3*s.* 6*d.*

This is the only complete English Edition sanctioned by the Author.

ENGLISH SONNETS. Collected and arranged by JOHN DENNIS. Small crown 8vo. Elegantly Bound. Price 3*s.* 6*d.*

HOME-SONGS FOR QUIET HOURS. By the Rev. Canon R. H. BAYNES, Editor of "English Lyrics" and "Lyra Anglicana." Handsomely printed and bound. Price 3*s.* 6*d.*

65, *Cornhill, &* 12, *Paternoster Row, London.*

DADDY'S PET. By NELSIE BROOK (MRS. ELLEN ROSS). Square crown 8vo, uniform with "Lost Gip." 6 Illustrations. Price One Shilling.

A pathetic story of lowly life, showing the good influence of home and of child-life upon an uncultivated but true-hearted "navvy."

LOST GIP. By HESBA STRETTON, Author of "Little Meg," "Alone in London," etc. Square crown 8vo. Six Illustrations. Price Eighteenpence.

"The story is a simple but most affecting one."—*Belfast News Letter.*

"The story is told most tenderly and touchingly."—*Literary Churchman.*

"The book is full of tender touches."—*Nonconformist.*

"Is an exquisitely touching little story, and amply sustains her high reputation."—*Church Herald.*

THE KING'S SERVANTS. By HESBA STRETTON, Author of "Lost Gip." Square crown 8vo, uniform with "Lost Gip." 8 Illustrations. Price Eighteenpence.

Part I.—FAITHFUL IN LITTLE. | Part II.—UNFAITHFUL. Part III.—FAITHFUL IN MUCH.

LOST GIP. Presentation Edition, Handsomely bound in square crown 4to, with Twelve Illustrations. Price 2s. 6d.

65, *Cornhill, & 12, Paternoster Row, London.*

SEEKING HIS FORTUNE, AND OTHER STORIES. Crown 8vo. Four Illustrations. Price 3*s.* 6*d.*

CONTENTS.

SEEKING HIS FORTUNE.   WHAT'S IN A NAME.
OLUF AND STEPHANOFF.   CONTRAST.
               ONESTA.

A series of instructive and interesting stories for children of both sexes, each one enforcing, indirectly, a good moral lesson.

THREE NEW STORIES. By MARTHA FARQUHARSON.

Each story is complete in itself, is elegantly bound, and illustrated. Price 3*s.* 6*d.*

I.

ELSIE DINSMORE. Crown 8vo, 3*s.* 6*d.*

II.

ELSIE'S GIRLHOOD. Crown 8vo, 3*s.* 6*d.*

III.

ELSIE'S HOLIDAYS AT ROSELANDS. Crown 8vo, 3*s.* 6*d.*

The Stories by this author have a very high reputation in America, and of all her books these are the most popular and widely circulated. These are the only English editions sanctioned by the author, who has a direct interest in this English Edition.

THE AFRICAN CRUISER. A Midshipman's Adventures on the West Coast. A Book for Boys. By S. WHITCHURCH SADLER, R.N. Illustrated. Crown 8vo. 3*s.* 6*d.*

A book of real adventures among slavers on the West Coast of Africa. One chief recommendation is the faithfulness of the local colouring.

65, *Cornhill,* & 12, *Paternoster Row, London.*

THE LITTLE WONDER-HORN. A Book of Child Stories. By JEAN INGELOW. Fifteen Illustrations. Cloth, gilt. 3s. 6d.

> " Full of fresh and vigorous fancy ; it is worthy of the author of some of the best of our modern verse."—*Standard.*
>
> "We like all the contents of the ' Little Wonder-Horn ' very much." —*Athenæum.*
>
> "We recommend it with confidence."—*Pall Mall Gazette.*

Second Edition.

BRAVE MEN'S FOOTSTEPS. A Book of Example and Anecdote for Young People. By the Editor of " Men who have Risen." With Four Illustrations, by C. DOYLE. 3s. 6d.

> " The little volume is precisely of the stamp to win the favour of those who, in choosing a gift for a boy, would consult his moral development as well as his temporary pleasure."—*Daily Telegraph.*
>
> " A readable and instructive volume."—*Examiner.*
>
> " No more welcome book for the schoolboy could be imagined."— *Birmingham Daily Gazette.*

Second Edition.

GUTTA-PERCHA WILLIE, THE WORKING GENIUS. By GEORGE MACDONALD. With Illustrations by ARTHUR HUGHES. Crown 8vo. 3s. 6d.

> " The cleverest child we know assures us she has read this story through five times. Mr. Macdonald will, we are convinced, accept that verdict upon his little work as final."—*Spectator.*

THE TRAVELLING MENAGERIE. By CHARLES CAMDEN, Author of "Hoity Toity." Illustrated by J. MAHONEY. Crown 8vo. 3s. 6d.

> " A capital little book . . . . deserves a wide circulation among our boys and girls."—*Hour.*
>
> " A very attractive story."—*Public Opinion.*

P LUCKY FELLOWS. A Book for Boys. By STEPHEN J. MAC KENNA. With Six Illustrations. Crown 8vo. Price 3*s*. 6*d*.

> "This is one of the very best 'Books for Boys' which have been issued this year."—*Morning Advertiser.*

> "A thorough book for boys . . . . written throughout in a manly straightforward manner that is sure to win the hearts of the children for whom it is intended."—*London Society.*

New Edition.

T HE DESERT PASTOR, JEAN JAROUSSEAU. Translated from the French of EUGENE PELLETAN. By COLONEL E. P. DE L'HOSTE. In fcap. 8vo, with an Engraved Frontispiece. Price 3*s*. 6*d*.

> "There is a poetical simplicity and picturesqueness; the noblest heroism; unpretentious religion; pure love, and the spectacle of a household brought up in the fear of the Lord. . . . The whole story has an air of quaint antiquity similar to that which invests with a charm more easily felt than described the site of some splendid ruin."—*Illustrated London News.*

> "This charming specimen of Eugène Pelletan's tender grace, humour, and high-toned morality."—*Notes and Queries.*

> "A touching record of the struggles in the cause of religious liberty of a real man."—*Graphic.*

T HE DESERTED SHIP. A Real Story of the Atlantic. By CUPPLES HOWE, Master Mariner. Illustrated by TOWNLEY GREEN. Crown 8vo. 3*s*. 6*d*.

> "Curious adventures with bears, seals, and other Arctic animals, and with scarcely more human Esquimaux, form the mass of material with which the story deals, and will much interest boys who have a spice of romance in their composition."—*Courant.*

H OITY TOITY, THE GOOD LITTLE FEL- LOW. By CHARLES CAMDEN. Illustrated. Crown 8vo. 3*s*. 6*d*.

> "Young folks may gather a good deal of wisdom from the story, which is written in an amusing and attractive style."—*Courant.*

> "Relates very pleasantly the history of a charming little fellow who meddles always with a kindly disposition with other people's affairs and helps them to do right. There are many shrewd lessons to be picked up in this clever little story."—*Public Opinion.*

65, *Cornhill, &* 12, *Paternoster Row, London.*

AT SCHOOL WITH AN OLD DRAGOON.
By STEPHEN J. MAC KENNA. Crown 8vo. 5*s*. With six
Illustrations. Price 5*s*.

> Stories of Military and Naval Adventure, related by a Retired Army
> Officer.

THE GREAT DUTCH ADMIRALS. By JACOB
DE LIEFDE. Crown 8vo. Illustrated. Price 5*s*.

> "A wholesome present for boys."—*Athenæum.*
> "A really excellent book."—*Spectator.*

Third Edition.

STORIES IN PRECIOUS STONES. By HELEN
ZIMMERN. With Six Illustrations. Crown 8vo. 5*s*.

> "A pretty little book which fanciful young persons will appreciate,
> and which will remind its readers of many a legend, and many an
> imaginary virtue attached to the gems they are so fond of wearing."—
> *Post.*

> "A series of pretty tales which are half fantastic, half natural, and
> pleasantly quaint, as befits stories intended for the young."—*Daily
> Telegraph.*

> "Certainly the book is well worth a perusal, and will not be soon laid
> down when once taken up."—*Daily Bristol Times.*

FANTASTIC STORIES. Translated from the
German of Richard Leander, by PAULINA B. GRANVILLE.
Crown 8vo. With six Illustrations, by M. E. Fraser-Tytler.
Price 5*s*.

> These are translations of some of the best of Richard Leander's well-
> known stories for children.

65, *Cornhill, &* 12, *Paternoster Row, London.*

TWO STORIES OF THE ANTIPODES.

THE TASMANIAN LILY. By JAMES BONWICK, Author of "Curious Facts of Old Colonial Days," &c. Crown 8vo. Illustrated. Price 5*s.*

"Many of his readers may be inclined to follow his advice, and without doubt to all intending emigrants the work will be found of great service, for not only is it well written, but every line bears the impress of having been written by an experienced and observant colonist."—*Morning Advertiser.*

"The characters of the story are capitally conceived and are full of hose touches which give them a natural appearance."—*Public Opinion.*

"Certainly attractive, and to those who have made up their mind to emigrate.'The Tasmanian Lily' will prove an interesting and useful book."—*Hour.*

MIKE HOWE, THE BUSHRANGER OF VAN DIEMEN'S LAND. By JAMES BONWICK, Author of "The Tasmanian Lily," &c. Crown 8vo. With a Frontispiece. Price 5*s.*

** Mr. Bonwick's wide Australasian knowledge has enabled him to produce a vivid and life-like historical story of the early days of the country.

SONGS FOR MUSIC. By FOUR FRIENDS. Square crown 8vo. Price 5*s.*

Containing Songs by—

STEPHEN H. GATTY.	REGINALD A. GATTY.
MRS. ALEXANDER EWING.	GREVILLE J. CHESTER.

LAYS OF A KNIGHT ERRANT IN MANY LANDS. By Major-General Sir VINCENT EYRE, C.B., K.C.S.I. Large Crown 8vo. Illustrated. Price 5*s.*

Lays of Pharaoh Land, of Wonder Land, of Home Land, and of Rhine Land, &c.

THE DAY OF REST. Volume for 1873, containing upwards of two hundred pictures by the best artists. Handsomely bound. Price 7s. 6d.

The following are among the contributors:—

His Grace the Archbishop of Canterbury,—the Right Rev. the Bishop of Winchester,—C. J. Vaughan, D.D., Master of the Temple,—the Rev. Thomas Binney,—the Rev. Hugh Stowell Brown,—Jean Ingelow,— Lady Verney,—Hesba Stretton,—Dora Greenwell,—C. C. Fraser-Tytler,—the Rev. A. W. Thorold,—the Rev. W. Fleming Stevenson,— the Rev. Professor Charteris,—Professor David Brown,—A. K. H. B.,— the Rev. Alexander Raleigh, D.D.,—the Very Rev. Dean Howson,— George Mac Donald,—the Author of "Episodes in an Obscure Life," —the Rev. R. W. Dale,—the Rev. J. Oswald Dykes, D.D.

ECHOES OF A FAMOUS YEAR. By HARRIET PARR, Author of "The Life of Jeanne d'Arc," "In the Silver Age," &c. Crown 8vo. 8s. 6d.

"A graceful and touching, as well as truthful account of the Franco-Prussian War. Those who are in the habit of reading books to children will find this at once instructive and delightful."—*Public Opinion.*

"Miss Parr has the great gift of charming simplicity of style; and if children are not interested in her book, many of their seniors will be."— *British Quarterly Review.*

THE PELICAN PAPERS. Reminiscences and Remains of a Dweller in the Wilderness. By JAMES ASHCROFT NOBLE. Crown 8vo. 6s.

"Written somewhat after the fashion of Mr. Helps's 'Friends in Council.'"—*Examiner.*

"Will well repay perusal by all thoughtful and intelligent readers."— *Liverpool Leader.*

"The 'Pelican Papers' make a very readable volume."—*Civilian.*

IN STRANGE COMPANY; OR, THE NOTE BOOK OF A ROVING CORRESPONDENT. By JAMES GREENWOOD, "The Amateur Casual." Crown 8vo. Price 6s.

These are some of the author's more recent experiences among the "Strange Company" of the Metropolis, which he chiefly found in the lower strata of Society. [*Just out.*

65, *Cornhill, & 12, Paternoster Row, London.*

'ILÂM ĔN NÂS. Historical Tales and Anecdotes of the Times of the Early Khalifahs. Translated from the Arabic Originals. By MRS. GODFREY CLERK, Author of "The Antipodes and Round the World." Crown 8vo. Price 7s.

"We have quoted enough to show that this is an unusually interesting book. The translation is the work of a lady, and a very excellent and scholar-like translation it is, clearly and pleasantly written, and illustrated and explained by copious notes, indicating considerable learning and research."—*Saturday Review.*

"Those who like stories full of the genuine colour and fragrance of the East, should by all means read Mrs. Godfrey Clerk's volume."—*Spectator.*

"On the whole, Mrs. Clerk's book, while it contains nothing that is not light and readable, will be found as full of valuable information as it is of amusing incident."—*Evening Standard.*

"The accomplished lady who presents us with the volume has illustrated and annotated the various stories very elaborately, and has succeeded in making them thoroughly intelligible; we think, indeed, that her notes form the most interesting part of the book."—*Literary Churchman.*

MOUNTAIN, MEADOW, AND MERE. A Series of Outdoor Sketches of Sport, Scenery, Adventures, and Natural History. By G. CHRISTOPHER DAVIES. With 16 Illustrations by W. HARCOURT. Crown 8vo. 6s.

MASTER-SPIRITS. By ROBERT BUCHANAN. Demy 8vo, 10s. 6d.

"GOOD BOOKS are the precious life-blood of MASTER-SPIRITS."—*Milton.*

These are some of the author's lighter and more generally interesting Essays on literary topics of permanent interest. His other prose contributions, critical and philosophical, to our literature are included in the collected editions of his works.

BRIEFS AND PAPERS. Being Sketches of the Bar and the Press. By TWO IDLE APPRENTICES. Crown 8vo. 7s. 6d.

"They are written with spirit and knowledge, and give some curious glimpses into what the majority will regard as strange and unknown territories."—*Daily News.*

"This is one of the best books to while away an hour and cause a generous laugh that we have come across for a long time."—*John Bull.*

65, *Cornhill, & 12, Paternoster Row, London.*

SOLDIERING AND SCRIBBLING. By ARCHIBALD FORBES, of the *Daily News*, Author of "My Experience of the War between France and Germany." Crown 8vo. 7s. 6d.

"All who open it will be inclined to read through for the varied entertainment which it affords."—*Daily News.*

"There is a good deal of instruction to outsiders touching military life in this volume."—*Evening Standard.*

"There is not a paper in the book which is not thoroughly readable and worth reading."—*Scotsman.*

STUDIES AND ROMANCES. By H. SCHÜTZ WILSON. 1 vol. Crown 8vo. Price 7s. 6d.

Shakespeare in Blackfriars.—The Loves of Goethe.—Romance of the Thames.—An Exalted Horn.—Two Sprigs of Edelweiss.—Between Moor and Main.—An Episode of the Terror.—Harry Ormond's Christmas Dinner.—Agnes Bernauerin.—"Yes" or "No"?—A Model Romance.—The Story of Little Jenny.—Dining.—The Record of a Vanished Life.

"Vivacious and interesting ; and the volume will certainly make one of the pleasantest that can be taken to the seaside or to any country place during holiday time."—*Scotsman.*

"We can cordially recommend this book to those of our readers who are about to rusticate or travel."—*Edin. Daily Review.*

"Open the book, however, at what page the reader may, he will find something to amuse and instruct, and he must be very hard to please if he finds nothing to suit him, either grave or gay, stirring or romantic, in the capital stories collected in this well-got-up volume."—*John Bull.*

"It contains several other capital descriptive sketches, and one or two interesting stories."—*Manchester Examiner.*

CABINET PORTRAITS. Biographical Sketches of Living Statesmen. By T. WEMYSS REID. 1 vol. crown 8vo. 7s. 6d.

"We have never met with a work which we can more unreservedly praise. The sketches are absolutely impartial."—*Athenæum.*

"We can heartily commend this work."—*Standard.*

"The 'Sketches of Statesmen' are drawn with a master hand."—*Yorkshire Post.*

Third Edition.

THE SECRET OF LONG LIFE. Dedicated by Special Permission to Lord St. Leonards. Large crown 8vo. 5*s.*

"A charming little volume, written with singular felicity of style and illustration."—*Times.*

"A very pleasant little book, which is always, whether it deal in paradox or earnest, cheerful, genial, scholarly."—*Spectator.*

"The bold and striking character of the whole conception is entitled to the warmest admiration."—*Pall Mall Gazette.*

"We should recommend our readers to get this book . . . . because they will be amused by the jovial miscellaneous and cultured gossip with which he strews his pages."—*British Quarterly Review.*

STREAMS FROM HIDDEN SOURCES. By B. MONTGOMERIE RANKING. Crown 8vo. 6*s.*

"In point of style it is well executed, and the prefatory notices are very good."—*Spectator.*

"The effect of reading the seven tales he presents to us is to make us wish for some seven more of the same kind."—*Pall Mall Gazette.*

"The tales are given throughout in the quaint version of the earliest English translators, and in the introduction to each will be found much curious information as to their origin, and the fate which they have met at the hands of later transcribers or imitators, and much tasteful appreciation of the varied sources from whence they are extracted. . . . . We doubt not that Mr. Ranking's enthusiasm will communicate itself to many of his readers, and induce them in like manner to follow back these streamlets to their parent river."—*Graphic.*

FOUR AMUSING TRAVEL-BOOKS.

I.

FAYOUM ; OR, ARTISTS IN EGYPT. A Tour with M. Gérôme and others. By J. LENOIR. Crown 8vo, cloth. Illustrated. 7*s. 6d.*

"The sketches, both by pen and pencil, are extremely interesting. Unlike books of travel of the ordinary kind, this volume is full of agreeable episodes told in a bright and sparkling style."

"A pleasantly written and very readable book."—*Examiner.*

"The book is very amusing. . . . Whoever may take it up will find he has with him a bright and pleasant companion."—*Spectator.*

65, Cornhill, & 12, Paternoster Row, London.

II.

A WINTER IN MOROCCO. By AMELIA PERRIER. Large crown 8vo. Illustrated. Price 10s. 6d.

"Well worth reading, and contains several excellent illustrations."—*Hour.*

"Miss Perrier is a very amusing writer. She has a good deal of humour, sees the oddity and quaintness (as they appear to us) of Oriental life with a quick observant eye, and evidently turned her opportunities of sarcastic examination to account."—*Daily News.*

"Her synonyms, her graphic touches, her *tours de phrase* on the subject of dirt, are admirable, and she happily succeeds in conveying such an impression of the horrors of the place, that none of the many artists who are good enough to paint those delightful slumberous interiors for us, all colour and grapes, moon-eyed beauties, glistening floors, diapered walls, and long-necked sherbet jars, will have a chance of being believed for the future."—*Spectator.*

III.

T ENT LIFE WITH ENGLISH GIPSIES IN NORWAY. By HUBERT SMITH. In 8vo, cloth. Five full-page Engravings, and 31 smaller Illustrations, with Map of the Country showing Routes. New Edition, revised and corrected. Price 21s.

"The work is copiously illustrated, not merely in name, but in fact; and there will be few who will not peruse it with pleasure."—*Standard.*

"If any of our readers think of scraping an acquaintance with Norway, let them read this book. The engravings are for the most part excellent. The gipsies, always an interesting study, become doubly interesting, when we are, as in these pages, introduced to them in their daily walk and conversation."—*Examiner.*

"Written in a very lively style, and has throughout a smack of dry humour and satiric reflection which shows the writer to be a keen observer of men and things. We hope that many will read it and find in it the same amusement as ourselves."—*Times.*

IV.

T HE PEARL OF THE ANTILLES; THE ARTIST IN CUBA. By WALTER GOODMAN. Crown 8vo. 7s. 6d.

"A good-sized volume, delightfully vivid and picturesque. . . . Several chapters devoted to the characteristics of the people are exceedingly interesting and remarkable. . . . The whole book deserves the heartiest commendation. . . . . Sparkling and amusing from beginning to end. Reading it is like rambling about with a companion who is content to loiter, observing everything, commenting upon everything, turning everything into a picture, with a cheerful flow of spirits, full of fun, but far above frivolity."—*Spectator.*

POETRY.

METRICAL TRANSLATIONS FROM THE GREEK AND LATIN POETS, AND OTHER POEMS. By R. B. BOSWELL, M.A. (Oxon). Crown 8vo. Price 5*s*.

ON VIOL AND FLUTE. A Volume of Lyrical Poems. By EDMUND W. GOSSE. With a Frontispiece by W. B. SCOTT. Small crown 8vo. Price 5*s*.

NARCISSUS AND OTHER POEMS. By E. CARPENTER. Small crown 8vo. Price 5*s*.

A TALE OF THE SEA, SONNETS, AND OTHER POEMS. By JAMES HOWELL. Crown 8vo, cloth, 5*s*.

IMITATIONS FROM THE GERMAN OF SPITTA AND TERSTEGEN. By LADY DURAND. Crown 8vo. 4*s*.

"An acceptable addition to the religious poetry of the day."— *Courant.*

POETRY—(*Continued*).

EASTERN LEGENDS AND STORIES IN ENGLISH VERSE. By LIEUTENANT NORTON POWLETT, Royal Artillery. Crown 8vo. 5s.

"Have we at length found a successor to Thomas Ingoldsby? We are almost inclined to hope so after reading 'Eastern Legends.' There is a rollicking sense of fun about the stories, joined to marvellous power of rhyming, and plenty of swing, which irresistibly reminds us of our old favourite."—*Graphic.*

EDITH; OR, LOVE AND LIFE IN CHESHIRE. By T. ASHE, Author of the "Sorrows of Hypsipylé," etc. Sewed. Price 6d.

"A really fine poem, full of tender, subtle touches of feeling."—*Manchester News.*

"Pregnant from beginning to end with the results of careful observation and imaginative power."—*Chester Chronicle.*

THE INN OF STRANGE MEETINGS, AND OTHER POEMS. By MORTIMER COLLINS. Crown 8vo. 5s.

"Abounding in quiet humour, in bright fancy, in sweetness and melody of expression, and, at times, in the tenderest touches of pathos."—*Graphic.*

"Mr. Collins has an undercurrent of chivalry and romance beneath the trifling vein of good-humoured banter which is the special characteristic of his verse. . . . The 'Inn of Strange Meetings' is a sprightly piece."—*Athenæum.*

THE GALLERY OF PIGEONS, AND OTHER POEMS. By THEO. MARZIALS. Crown 8vo. 4s. 6d.

"A conceit abounding in prettiness."—*Examiner.*

"Contains as clear evidence as a book can contain that its composition was a source of keen and legitimate enjoyment. The rush of fresh, sparkling fancies is too rapid, too sustained, too abundant, not to be spontaneous."—*Academy.*

POETRY—*(Continued)*.

GOETHE'S FAUST. A NEW Translation in Rime.
By the REV. C. KEGAN PAUL. Crown 8vo. 6*s.*

"His translation is the most minutely accurate that has yet been produced. . . . Has special merits of its own, and will be useful and welcome to English students of Goethe."—*Examiner.*

"Mr. Paul evidently understands 'Faust,' and his translation is as well suited to convey its meaning to English readers as any we have yet seen."—*Edinburgh Daily Review.*

"Mr. Paul is a zealous and a faithful interpreter."—*Saturday Review.*

CALDERON'S DRAMAS.
THE PURGATORY OF ST. PATRICK.
THE WONDERFUL MAGICIAN.
LIFE IS A DREAM.

Translated from the Spanish. By DENIS FLORENCE MAC-CARTHY. 10*s.*

These translations have never before been published. The "Purgatory of St. Patrick" is a new version, with new and elaborate historical notes.

WALLED IN, AND OTHER POEMS. By the REV. HENRY J. BULKELEY. Crown 8vo. 5*s.*

"A remarkable book of genuine poetry which will be welcome to all lovers of the Muse."—*Evening Standard.*

"'Walled in' is a lyrical monologue, in which an imprisoned nun, distracted with suffering and passion, tells the story of her love and the terrible punishment it brought upon herself and her lover. There is genuine power displayed in this poem, and also in another of a similar cast, entitled 'Not an Apology.'"—*Examiner.*

". . . Describes with great felicity strong human emotions, as well as the varied aspects of nature. . . . . In a very different style, but one familiar to us of late years, the writer relates in blank verse a simple story called 'The Hat-band.' Poetical feeling is manifest here, and the diction of the poem is unimpeachable."—*Pall Mall Gazette.*

POETRY—(*Continued*).

SONNETS, LYRICS, AND TRANSLATIONS.
By the REV. C. TENNYSON TURNER.   Crown 8vo. 4s. 6d.

"Mr. Turner is a genuine poet; his song is sweet and pure, beautiful in expression, and often subtle in thought."—*Pall Mall Gazette.*

"The dominant charm of all these sonnets is the pervading presence of the writer's personality, never obtruded but always impalpably diffused. The light of a devout, gentle, and kindly spirit, a delicate and graceful fancy, a keen intelligence irradiates these thoughts."

"Mr. Turner's rare skill as a painter of landscape is the characteristic that will be likely to excite most attention. With an eye prompt to catch the rich varieties of form and gradations of colour in nature, he unites a hand apt at rendering either her breadth or her delicacy."—*Contemporary Review.*

SONGS OF LIFE AND DEATH. By JOHN
PAYNE, Author of "Intaglios," "Sonnets," "The Masque of Shadows," etc.   Crown 8vo. 5s.

"The art of ballad-writing has long been lost in England, and Mr. Payne may claim to be its restorer. It is a perfect delight to meet with such a ballad as 'May Margaret' in the present volume."—*Westminster Review.*

SONGS OF TWO WORLDS. By a NEW WRITER.
Fcap. 8vo, cloth, 5s.   Second Edition.

"The 'New Writer' is certainly no tyro. No one after reading the first two poems, almost perfect in rhythm and all the graceful reserve of true lyrical strength, can doubt that this book is the result of lengthened thought and assiduous training in poetical form. . . . These poems will assuredly take high rank among the class to which they belong."—*British Quarterly Review, April 1st.*

"If these poems are the mere preludes of a mind growing in power and in inclination for verse, we have in them the promise of a fine poet. . . . The verse describing Socrates has the highest note of critical poetry."—*Spectator, February 17th.*

"Are we in this book making the acquaintance of a fine and original poet, or of a most artistic imitator? And our deliberate opinion is that the former hypothesis is the right one. It has a purity and delicacy of feeling like morning air."—*Graphic, March 16th.*

POETRY—(*Continued*).

EROS AGONISTES. By E. B. D. Crown 8vo, 3s. 6d.

"The author of these verses has written a very touching story of the human heart in the story he tells with such pathos and power, of an affection cherished so long and so secretly. . . . It is not the least merit of these pages that they are everywhere illumined with moral and religious sentiment suggested, not paraded, of the brightest, purest character."—*Standard*.

THE DREAM AND THE DEED, AND OTHER POEMS. By PATRICK SCOTT, Author of "Footpaths between Two Worlds," etc. Fcap. 8vo, cloth, 5s.

"A bitter and able satire on the vice and follies of the day, literary, social, and political."—*Standard*.

"Shows real poetic power coupled with evidences of satirical energy."—*Edinburgh Daily Review*.

THE LEGENDS OF ST. PATRICK AND OTHER POEMS. By AUBREY DE VERE. Crown 8vo. 5s.

"Mr. De Vere's versification in his earlier poems is characterised by great sweetness and simplicity. He is master of his instrument, and rarely offends the ear with false notes. Poems such as these scarcely admit of quotation, for their charm is not, and ought not to be, found in isolated passages; but we can promise the patient and thoughtful reader much pleasure in the perusal of this volume."—*Pall Mall Gazette*.

"We have marked, in almost every page, excellent touches from which we know not how to select. We have but space to commend the varied structure of his verse, the carefulness of his grammar, and his excellent English. All who believe that poetry should raise and not debase the social ideal, all who think that wit should exalt our standard of thought and manners, must welcome this contribution at once to our knowledge of the past and to the science of noble life."—*Saturday Review*.

POETRY—(*Continued*).

THE POETICAL AND PROSE WORKS OF ROBERT BUCHANAN. A Collected Edition, in 5 vols.

VOL. I. CONTAINS :—
BALLADS AND ROMANCES. | BALLADS AND POEMS OF LIFE.

VOL. II. CONTAINS :—
BALLADS AND POEMS OF LIFE. | ALLEGORIES AND SONNETS.

VOL. III. CONTAINS :—
CRUISKEEN SONNETS. | BOOK OF ORM. | POLITICAL MYSTICS.

The Contents of the remaining Volumes will be duly announced.

VIGNETTES IN RHYME, AND VERS DE SOCIÉTÉ. Collected Verses. By AUSTIN DOBSON. Crown 8vo. Price 5*s.*

" His ' Vignettes ' are really clever, clear-cut, and careful."— *Athenæum.*

" We were hardly prepared for the touches of genuine beauty which adorn so many of these little poems."—*Spectator.*

THE DISCIPLES. A New Poem. By HARRIET ELEANOR HAMILTON KING, Author of " Aspromonte and other Poems." Crown 8vo. Price 7*s.* 6*d.*

The present work was commenced at the express instance of the great Italian patriot, Mazzini, and commemorates some of his associates and fellow workers—men who looked up to him as their master and teacher. The author enjoyed the privilege of Mazzini's friendship, and the first part of this work was on its way to him when tidings reached this country that he had passed away.

65, Cornhill, & 12, Paternoster Row, London.

POETRY—(*Continued*).

S ONGS FOR SAILORS. By Dr. W. C. BENNETT. Dedicated by Special Request to H.R.H. the Duke of Edinburgh. Crown 8vo. 3s. 6d. With Steel Portrait and Illustrations.

An Edition in Illustrated paper Covers. Price 1s.

A SPROMONTE AND OTHER POEMS. Second Edition, cloth. 4s. 6d.

"The volume is anonymous, but there is no reason for the author to be ashamed of it. The 'Poems of Italy' are evidently inspired by genuine enthusiasm in the cause espoused; and one of them, 'The Execution of Felice Orsini,' has much poetic merit, the event celebrated being told with dramatic force."—*Athenæum.*

"The verse is fluent and free."—*Spectator.*

T HOUGHTS IN VERSE. By E. B. Small crown 8vo. Price 1s. 6d.

*** This is a Collection of Verses expressive of religious feeling, written from a Theistic stand-point.

Just out.

C OSMOS. A POEM. Small crown 8vo. Price 3s. 6d. Subject—

NATURE IN THE PAST AND IN THE PRESENT. MAN IN THE PAST AND IN THE PRESENT. THE FUTURE.

65, Cornhill, & 12, Paternoster Row, London.

THE CORNHILL LIBRARY OF FICTION.

3s. 6d. per volume.

It is intended in this Series to produce books of such merit that readers will care to preserve them on their shelves. They are well printed on good paper, handsomely bound, with a Frontispiece, and are sold at the moderate price of **3s. 6d. each.**

FOR LACK OF GOLD. By CHARLES GIBBON.

GOD'S PROVIDENCE HOUSE. By MRS. G. L. BANKS.

ROBIN GRAY. By CHARLES GIBBON. With a Frontispiece by Hennessy.

KITTY. By MISS M. BETHAM-EDWARDS.

READY MONEY MORTIBOY. A Matter-of-Fact Story.

HIRELL. By JOHN SAUNDERS, Author of "Abel Drake's Wife."

ONE OF TWO. By J. HAIN FRISWELL, Author of "The Gentle Life," etc.

ABEL DRAKE'S WIFE. By JOHN SAUNDERS.

OTHER STANDARD NOVELS TO FOLLOW.

65, Cornhill, & 12, Paternoster Row, London.